UNREMARKABLE
IN LIGHT

Christine Falk

to the Doc
with healing hands
and a patient heart

authorHOUSE®

Christine Falk

AuthorHouse™
1663 Liberty Drive
Bloomington, IN 47403
www.authorhouse.com
Phone: 1-800-839-8640

First published by AuthorHouse 7/11/2011

ISBN: 978-1-4567-4980-4 (e)
ISBN: 978-1-4567-4978-1 (hc)
ISBN: 978-1-4567-4979-8 (sc)

Library of Congress Control Number: 2011904656

Printed in the United States of America

FOR LARRY

CHAPTER ONE

"I don't talk much. I'm not a talker."

"It's O.K. uncle, he's not the chatty kind."

"I like things quiet. I'm used to having peace and quiet. He shouldn't be too chatty." The voice is gruff and rasping, low. He sounds older than his forty years.

Ben speculates inwardly if leaving his six year old son James with his uncle Earl is a big mistake. The man has always been somewhat inept socially; sheltered, solitary, and unsocial. His behaviour always appears to Ben to be more suitable of an awkward introvert teenager and not a forty year old man. In Ben's point of view Earl provokes a fond image of bumbling awkwardness. Still he trusts this man implicitly, loves him like a brother, and know his son will be in caring hands while he stays here.

Ben's child, James, slight and pallid, has experienced an exceptionally hard year. He seems overly reserved and closed off most of the time. Ben feels that it is very untypical of a six year old to be so reserved, definitely not chatty. On the other hand, Ben reasons, these two are a lot alike; quiet, thoughtful, humble. Besides, he tells himself, he can't allow himself to think of it as a mistake when it's his only available option.

"Thought they were all chatty." Earl is gruff but warm as he slurps large sips from a nearly empty beer can. "Don't all kids chatter?"

Ben examines Earls appearance as he considers this question. A mass of dark curls tangles up from beneath the blue ball cap and hangs low enough to curl against a worn denim shirt collar. Dark round eyes appear somehow innocent and yet guarded, veiled by sweeping dark lashes. Earl's expression is often stern but always a warmth exudes in his eyes and at the corners of his mouth. Even in light-heartedness Ben see a hidden sadness behind Earl's infrequent smiles. Earl has been sad for as long as Ben can remember. It was never so much a statement as a attachment that followed him where-ever he went.

"No uncle, not this one anyway. Mom always said he has an old soul. She said she could see it in his eyes."

Ben exposes his grief for his late mother in a sudden solemn lowness. His shoulders sag and his eyes avert to the dust on his shoes with the deep tilt of his weary head. His mother had always been that place of anchor for Ben when life's storms blew in. Losing her earlier in the year has been the biggest loss of his life until now.

James had suffered his gramma's death especially hard. He had been inconsolably despondent for days, retreated and curled up like a wounded animal. Ben recalls how Earl had also voiced a deep loss at her passing and had shut himself off from the outside world for a time after the funeral, just like the child. Ben's hope is that these unusual similarities provide Earl and James with a base from which they can build some level of compassion towards each other in the time they will be together.

James is a skinny child with hair like old straw. He appears delicate, in stark contrast to Ben's curly haired, thick wristed and broad shouldered, bloke of an uncle. The boy shuffles toward the wooden steps of the log home, halts at the bottom, and peers up at uncle Earl. The two have never formally met until today. Today they will begin living under the same roof. Together they will live under Earl's roof.

"You got room for me Sir?" he whispers, hoisting his small blue suitcase closer to his chest. Both clenched hands wrapped around the faded blue handle.

"Sad about your mother. How long has it been?" Earl speaks low and mumbled, still addressing Ben.

Ben hesitates. It is an awkward moment deciding weather to address the question about his mother's passing or to question Earl's seeming indifference to his little son. Was he a fool to think this could work? However temporary could this arrangement possibly do more harm than good? He wonders to himself ever second guessing this decision.

There is a deep cool breath between them before Earl drearily answers his own question, "about seven months. Terrible loss."

The two men watch, arms crossed in dour thoughts of Ben's mother Grace, both looking down from the porch, as the child struggles up each of the steps with his bag. Tiny soft pink fingers wrap around the plastic handle. He holds it high and close to his chest. A slight breeze shifts his fair hair as he takes each step. Neither man makes any sympathetic motion to unburden the child. James appears unhurried, tired and weary as he climbs, then he halts a breath too near to the big man. His neck is strained, his chin turns sharply upward as he addresses Earl.

"Brought my own blanket an' pillow there in that sack my dad is holding." Struggling boldly to look up at the man's face, there is resignation and acceptance in his small features tempered by a slight apprehension. His weariness is greatly evident in his mumbled voice and in his tired eyes. Weary not just from the drive, but from the many troubled days that preceded this one.

"Been a long drive Uncle Earl." an equal measure of resign is heard in Ben's dulled point. "Nine hours. Long day for us both."

The climate between them is shaded in deep blue weariness and the many things Ben feels are better left unsaid. There is so much that he simply has no words to express at this moment. The wind is warm on his face but sets a chill down his back, he shivers. His own sense of hopelessness is weighted beneath sleepless nights and endless days that seem to continually swirl uncontrollably around him.

"Come on in then." Earl motions as he turns to the door and leads the way inside. The three move from the grey brown wooden plank steps of the rustic log cabin and enter Earl's modest home.

"It's a bit dark." The child notes with a slight smile of approval before Earl switches on a lamp near the sofa.

Ben can't help but puzzle at his son's peculiarity. The child's reactions are never what he expects. Always he had imagined having a bright cheery child and not this increasingly introverted little man older and sadder than his short years. James is darkly serious with unusual eccentricities. He is happy to stay indoors on the sunniest days and finds solitary amusements that would bore most other boys his age. Ben hopes this change, this new environment, will be a positive influence. So far the realization of those hopes seems rather bleak. He knows that Earl is somewhat of an outdoorsman and that James will be spending more time out of the house while he is staying at Earl's. He feels that any change has got to be an improvement. Also, there is at times nothing left in him but hope. He wants that for his son as well, some reason to hope and dream of sunny happy days ahead as children should.

"I got this extra room." Earl says, finally speaking to the child directly. He crosses the living room and leads the boy towards the back of the house. His focus has shifted entirely from Ben to James as though the inside comforts of his home have expanded his warmth towards the child. "Small room. Not too big."

"I'm not too big Sir."

James is still struggling with the burden of the hard shell suitcase with the rounded plastic corners but does not ask for help. He hastens to follow as the small piece of luggage knocks against his knees with every step.

"The room used to belong to my dog Prince. I had to move some things around."

Earl pushes open the Pine wood bedroom door and stands aside so that the boy may enter first. The room is almost barren, clean and uncluttered. Sparsely decorated yet warm and inviting to the boy. The denim curtains and bedspread are complimented by the navy blue area rug placed on the wooden floor between the single bed and the pine dresser.

"There's a dresser and a bed. I put a rug down." Earl points out these obvious features. The room, like Earl, is ordinary and plain. The walls are bare of any decorations except for a Fountain Tire calendar hung near the window.

"It's fine." James responds softly with a trace of resignation and an accepting nod. "It's just fine."

Earl likes that the child is polite and respectful. He very much appreciates that James is a child of few words although he had expected the child to be more lively and chatty. There is a sober reserved blankness in the boy's expression and his movements. Can't read his mood just now, sort of nondescript, like he is weighing out some sort of decision or evaluation. Earl is glad that his new "room mate" appears to be an unobtrusive sort. Not chatty.

"I'll leave you to unpack."

"Thank you." James is dour, almost dismissive.

For a moment Earl wonders why someone so small would be so solemn, so earnest. Then for the fist time in a very long time he allows himself memories, with deep angst, of the difficulties of his own childhood. Memories long buried and hidden. Momentarily caught in uncomfortable thoughts too dismal to speak of, he personally identifies with these manners typical of a discontent existence. The child's movements are slow, each one seeming deliberate and measured. James seems especially shielding and possessive of his few belongings as his small delicate hands handle each item with resolute care. Yes, Earl confirms inwardly, here we have an old soul. An old and already weary soul in an especially weary little package.

Watching from the door Earl observes James removing his crumpled belongings from the small piece of luggage with the plastic handle as he places them in the wooden three drawer dresser. Shirts and pants, socks and sweaters. A photo of James and his father Ben, in a red plastic frame, is placed on the barren window ledge near to the bed. Four picture books and a stuffed bear, a note pad and a package of coloured pencils, all laid out on the bedspread, then the child closes his travel case and slips it underneath the bed.

There is a deeply quiet resolve to his actions that Earl feels a growing awareness for. Sadly Earl can only speculate at the troubled storm of emotions James might be weathering beneath this tired and serene exterior. He has been privy to the details of some of James and Ben's recent troubles through brief telephone conversations had with Ben and can only speculate at the unseen scars those trials have left on the soul and spirit of this innocent little man.

CHAPTER TWO

BACK IN THE LIVING room Ben is looking at a faded photo of Earl's mother Ella that is hanging on the wall above Earl's denim chocolate brown cloth sofa. Ella is a young mother in the photo, sitting tall in a ladder back wooden chair in a sunny yellow blouse, an infant on her lap and a young brooding adolescent standing at her side. The older child seems to resemble her own geometric features more than the smaller child who is round and plump with youthfulness and has unruly dark curly hair. Ella's straight brown shoulder length hair is not yet greying and her skin is clear and bright. She is smiling openly, cheerfully. The child in her lap is laughing, mouth open, eyes smiling. The photo backdrop is a pale blue bed sheet. The photo frame is wooden, probably pine, but with a deep cherry stain.

"I don't remember her Earl, your mother. I do remember stories my mom would tell me about her. Mom described her as a home body, quiet. Mom always said she liked to cook and bake birthday cakes, and she loved animals. Stuff like that right?"

"Yeah, stuff like that." A sadness hangs on Earl's words. He is uncomfortable with resurrecting images from the past. Earl rarely speaks of his mother or his childhood. Ben has made mention of both of their mothers in the short time he has been here. It has been such a long time, years, since Earl has discussed any of his past with anyone at all. His inner voice aches at the old skeletons that are smoothly emerging through Ben's words, dusty and shadowy memories long buried by time and long silent. Ben's back is to Earl and he doesn't see the furrowed brow of Earl's dulled underlying heartache.

If he would turn and look he might identify, even in this dim lighting, Earl's long buried anguish in a deeply creased forehead. Earl would prefer to leave his memories in the darker shadows of the past. He sees no good to come from speaking about the earlier, less than happy, period of his life. Still, Ben carries the conversation forward.

"You had a dog uncle Earl, Prince. Right? Prince, was that his name?"

"Prince was a great dog. My best friend growing up. I had Prince a long time." At mention of the dearly loved dog his edge softens.

"Wasn't he a Collie?"

"Sheppard,. Sheppard mixed with other stuff." Earl recalls with fond affection.

Ben now detects the slightest change in Earls voice, softened and more relaxed at the mention of the pet. He turns and looks at the older man. Earl appears tired but more youthful in the softened living room lighting. Ben wonders if he could keep going on the subject but because he feels a cool sadness behind Earl's expression he lets it go. Not too eager to discuss his own sad situation either Ben chooses to leave it all hanging in the air and steps to the opposite side of the room. His abrupt action seems elusive, almost as though he is physically hurrying away from the sound of his own voice. The empty break in the conversation feels just as strained as all the unspoken truths the two men anguish to avoid.

"I thought I'd stay over and head back to the city in the morning if that's alright. That'll help James get settled in."

"I'm settled in just fine." James timidly mumbles as he emerges from the bedroom. He crosses the living room to his dad and takes the sack with his Batman blanket and pillow. His footsteps fall without a sound leaving not a trace of existence like a small sad ghost as he disappears again down the short hall to the bedroom.

Earl moves soft footed and just as soundlessly to the kitchen. He turns on the light that hangs over the wooden table, steps to the refrigerator and takes out a frosted chocolate cake that his neighbour Amber has brought over in anticipation of Earl's house guests. He cuts three pieces, placing them on torn white paper towel squares laid on the table. The feel of the living room has gotten uncomfortably cool and itchy. The kitchen, now flooded in yellow brightness, seems more inviting now. Next he pours a small glass of milk and gets out two beers from the bottom shelf of the fridge.

As he closes the fridge door Earl turns and mutely offers a beer to Ben, waving the brown bottle in the air. A defensive peace offering of sorts in an unspoken and invisible clash. He pulls out a wooden chair from the kitchen table and motions for Ben to join him.

The two men sit silent in their thoughts and sip their beers. Ben is tired from the drive and from the regrettable reasons for his having to be here. His reasons are his missing wife and a need to temporarily place James in Earl's safe care while he irons out the wrinkles that have enveloped his life. Earl is also deep in thought, wondering if he is capable to care for a small child, imagining a comparison to keeping a pet or to maintaining his truck. Having never cared for a child Earl is optimistically hopeful that James will tell him what is needed or wanted from the boy.

The beers are half finished before James emerges from his newly appointed room having arranged all of his things to his liking. The child's eyes light up at the sight of the cake and milk there on the table for him. Without one word he sits, then anxiously looks to his dad and his uncle Earl. Earl gives the boy a nod to go ahead, and James immediately devours the cake slice and washes it down with the entire glass of milk in one tip.

"More? Is there more please?" Splinters of longing and buoyancy expose in the child's eyes and voice without apology breaking the quiet in the air. Ben puzzles again at the boy, now interacting with a greater measure of normalcy, happy behaviours he would welcome from a son. It is as though a switch had be switched and the shy introvert has all of a sudden vanished. Ben is confused by his son, not recognizing the weight of influence a wedge of cake might have on a little boy.

Earl pushes his own untouched piece of cake across the smooth wooden table top and reaches for the milk that is still at hand on the counter. He pours the small glass full again. In the time it takes Ben to take two bites of his cake James' second piece has disappeared. James, hopeful, glances once more at Earl. The old guy shakes his head "no", his dark curls bounce unruly with the gesture, and James nods in response with a gloomy sullenness mixed with muted gratefulness. He sips the second glass of milk much slower.

"Getting near bed time, best hold off." Earl offers without having any idea why this reasoning should have effect. He just thinks it is what a responsible uncle ought to say.

Ben finishes his cake and wipes the crumbs from his mouth with the paper towel napkin. "You sure ate that fast. A lot faster than potatoes or spinach."

James stares up at his dad with an annoyed mixture of disbelief and awe at his fathers apparent lack of common sense. "Dad ...... ," he states matter-of-factly as though bothered at having to explain the obvious, "I just like cake."

Earl voices agreement with a hint of amusement. "Who doesn't like cake?"

The three sit and talk for a while, conversation punctuated with briefs of quiet contemplation. Earl tells them about the neighbour lady, Amber, who will watch James while he is at work. Ben talks about the divorce lawyer and the realtor he has hired but avoids mention of his wife directly. He does slip in mention of a police officer by name, a missing persons detective.

James does not understand anything about lawyers but wonders out loud about when the police men will find his missing mother. Not surprising to the child his questions hang unanswered and are quietly ignored. He has become accustomed to questions about his mother being left in the air. When his further probe of the subject continues to go unanswered he inquires if there are other kids around, but with an air of indifference as if he would be fine with either. Being alone here or making new friends, one way or the other makes little difference and he doesn't even know how long he will be here. He has gotten accustomed to being alone, not having friends to play with. Would never admit that it bothers him, he only thinks that would be a bother for his dad. Having friends of his own would have definitely been a bother for his mother.

Earl changes the subject to recollections about his home town as Ben might remember from his childhood. It is now a town where children grow up and move away and farmers die on unproductive farmland. There are more rig hands than farm hands living in the area now, a common sign of the changing times. Earl makes brief mention of Ben's dad, Ben Wallace Senior, but the topic is short lived since Ben's memories of his father are as dusty and faded as a dirt road. Ben's father had left his life long ago when

Ben was a teenager. The only Ben Wallace that James has ever know is his own father sitting next to him at the table.

After the beers Earl gathers a blanket and pillow to give Ben for sleeping on the couch. James washes up and puts on his pyjamas, then climbs up into the bed in his new room under the Batman covers he has laid out over the warm blue denim quilt.

The men say good night, Ben kisses James on the forehead. Earl does not, instead he pats the child on the head like he would do to an obedient dog. They leave the room and close the door. Earl allows Ben to leave ahead of him. He then takes a step back and opens the boy's bedroom door just a bit so that the light from the bathroom across the hall will shine in. "Just a little light, just in case." he reasons.

Milk is put back in the fridge, lights are turned down in the kitchen, and Earl heads down the hallway for his own bedroom at the back of the house. Murmured thoughts from his own past and his own troubled childhood are now awakened and whisper to him as he lays his head on his firm pillow. He had not expected these emotions to surface from the dark places of his past. They are like a tree rooted outside a window with branches scratching at the glass. It is impossible to uproot or to remove, it is practically a living part of the structure. As Earl's eyes close he tells himself he will simply have to get accustomed to that scratching, subtle voice from seeds planted long ago.

CHAPTER THREE

IT IS EARL'S SEVENTH birthday and all week his older brother Art has been indiscreetly dropping lame useless hints about how great Earl's birthday present is. Although the many hints have done little to enlighten Earl he is literally bursting with excitement. He is little, very small for his age, and not very bright; that's what he thinks he hears the first grade teacher often says, but he knows enough. He knows his mother is poor and gets Welfare from the government and that he should not hope for fancy expensive things. Not even for his birthday.

Earl's brother Art is a lot older than he is, eleven years older, and doesn't spend much time with him. He's eighteen and going to graduate from high school very soon. Art says that after graduation he is getting a job and moving far away from here.

Earl can't imagine why anyone would want to leave here except that they are poor and always having to "make do" as his mother says. Earl sometimes thinks about how life will be without his big brother around. Sure Art picks on him some, but sometimes they get along good and even do fun things together. Art even let's Earl help him work on his old car and second hand dirt bike. Art has always been Earl's help with school work and his defender in the playground. Soon it will just be Earl and his mom.

"O.K. Earl come sit here." Ella motions. "Here at the head of the table. That's where the birthday boy should sit. It's time for cake. Cake then presents."

"Yeah cake." Everyone cheers.

There is Earl and his mom Ella, and his brother Art of course. Also good friends from down the road, Maria and her son Frank, and her teenaged daughter Grace. Frank is only five years old but kind of fun to have around, even if his mom still washes his face for him. Grace is fifteen and Earl believes she is the prettiest girl he has ever seen in his life, except he don't want anyone to know he likes a girl. She is a thin girl with long hair that she never ever ties back, and soft brown eyes with long eyelashes, and sweet pink lips that are always smiling at everyone. Maybe when he's older and bigger he could tell her how nice he thinks she is but not today with everyone gathering together in the kitchen.

Earl's mom lights the seven candles on his cake, the little ones with the colour and white spiralled down the length of them lightly stabbed into blue frosting. Earl's candles are five of the blue and two of the yellow and none of the pink ones. Art says boys don't like pink and Art knows a lot of stuff like that.

Ella carries the made from scratch cake into the dinning room as the rest of the group sing the "Happy Birthday" song. They all enjoy cake and drink orange juice, the kind made from powder drink crystals. Earl had really hoped for pop today, he likes Grape, but he knows it's expensive and his mom says it makes him too hyper, so he didn't bother to ask. Lucky to have such a nice cake with frosting he figures.

The mood in the home is joyous and very casual. The group are happily eating and laughing around the old chrome table with the yellowed melamine top. Sitting on Ella's mismatched wooden chairs.

As they finish their birthday cake Earl observes his mom lean over to whisper something to Grace, then Grace goes outside and returns a moment later with a large cardboard box. She is exceptionally careful as she sets it down on the floor next to the table. Her movements are cautious and gentle, she tries not to tip it to one side or the other. Earl is disappointed that it's not wrapped with fancy paper. What good could possibly be inside a plain cardboard box?

"You already brought a present Grace, it's right there on the counter."

"Yeah I know we brought that one Earl," she answers, "this big one is from your mom."

"Mom and me." Art injects, hurt to be left out of the credit. Earl is just slightly saddened that his mom and brother did not bother to wrap his birthday gift.

"Open ours first Earl." Frank bounces in his chair, cake crumbs spewing from his lips. "Open ours, open ours."

Ella furtively steals a glance at Grace. Grace answers her questioning eyes wordlessly with the thumbs up signal then motions a sleepy sort of motion with the back of her hand against her cheek as she tilts her head to one side. Art and Maria both nod and smile, only Earl and Frank miss the meaning behind the gesture.

"Finish your cake Frank, and please chew with your mouth closed." Maria gently pleads as she grabs a paper towel from the table. She spit's on it a little to moisten it, and wipes her five year old son's face.

Earl watches in disgust, "how embarrassing" he muses.

Art passes the neighbours gift across the table to Earl. Excited little hands tear impatiently at the bright and colourful race car pattern wrapping paper and his tight brown curls bounce around his smiling face. Remembering his manners he stops to look at the card, giving it a quick glance and a nod, then continues his destruction of the gift wrap and box.

"Wow a Tonka dump truck! And wait, there's more, a set of tools. Oh Wow, Thanks you guys." Earl gushes.

They are small pretend little kid tools, Earl knows this. He has seen the big tools that Art has and like Frank's dad has in his shop. But wow is he happy to get tools.

"Wow am I happy..... You guys are the best. I wanted tools a long time, didn't I say I wanted tools Art? Tools for my very own, thanks. And this truck is the best."

He bursts from his chair and runs around the table to hug them all, Maria, Frank, and Grace. He hugs Grace tightest but not too long cause if he did his big brother would tease him about having a crush. Earl isn't entirely sure what a crush is but he thinks it's the warm feeling he gets when he hugs Grace, and when she smiles at him, and when she's nice to him and Frank, which is always. Grace is always nice to them even though she's lots older. Not like Art, Art is mostly unpleasant and likes to tease because he is older and smarter and knows lots of stuff that Earl don't know.

Earl is climbing back up onto his chair to play with his tools when there is a strange noise inside the big brown cardboard box on the floor. He was so excited at having received the truck and tools from his friends that he all but forgot about the box, the present from his mom and brother Art, which Art says is awesome and he's really gonna love.

There's another sound like a muffled whimper, and then some scratching. Earl can't begin to imagine that he's getting what he is beginning to guess is in that big box because it's alive and moving in there and sounds just like Earl imagined something like what he is guessing might sound. His face is frozen in surprise and delight, eyes wide and mouth agape. Then another whimper, and then a little brown paw pushes through the box top. Then there is a barely audible bark, and the room fills with laughter as Earl falls off his chair at the sight of the little brown nose of the puppy shoving his way out of the box.

The little brown pup pushes through the cardboard box flaps and jumps out, and then Earl and the little dog are rolling on the floor. Frank joins them on the linoleum. The pup licks at Franks face which is once again covered with cake and frosting. Children and puppy frolic excitedly on the dining room floor of the cozy old farm house.

"Looks like somebody finally woke up." Grace cheers.

"Is he mine mom? Is he really mine?"

"Of course he is, it is your birthday isn't it?"

"I get to keep him? Really?"

"Yes Earl, he's yours. He's all yours. Yours to keep." she confirms again happily.

"How we gonna feed him? Do I have to get a job? What's he gonna eat mom?"

"A job." Ella laughs, "You don't have to get a job Earl. Don't you worry about that." The dog cost her nothing, but inside she is bothered that her constant financial worries have infused a dim dose of hardship into the little boy's insights. She wishes her young child did not have such understanding for the reality of their disadvantaged life.

"We'll figure it out. Your brother's going away soon so that's going to be one less mouth to feed at the table, and dogs eat table scraps and stuff like that. We'll make do."

"I thought the scraps were for the barn animals. Hey. Do dogs eat peas and spinach?" he asks hopefully.

"No, not that I know of but they eat meat scraps and we'll buy him dog food too. Don't worry Earl, he is your dog to keep. All yours."

"Hey Earl …. what …. what you gonna name him?" Frank asks between breaths as the excited little puppy licks unrelentingly at his face and hands. "He's gotta have a good name." Frank breaths cake crumbs, warm and moist, closely into his friends face as the puppy scrambles happily between them.

"Oh, I know this. I been dreaming of having a dog for a long time, and when I get one I know his name is gonna be Prince. I seen a movie once with a dog name of Prince. It was the best dog ever. My dog's name is Prince. Prince for sure. Thanks mom, this is the best day ever in my whole life."

That night Prince, a Sheppard cross mutt, sleeps with Earl, and then again the next night. When Ella suggests the dog sleep outside, or at least in the porch she is met with objection by both the boy and the little dog. After that it is established that Earl's room is now also Prince's room, and where ever Earl goes Prince also goes like a lovely furry shadow.

It is a relief to Earl's mom Ella a few weeks later that Earl has the dog as a companion when her oldest son Art follows through on his own plans and moves out on his own after his high school graduation. The boy and dog become inseparable throughout the long hot summer month. They are together every moment of every day. It is a royal battle when September comes and Earl has to begin another year of school.

Prince steadfastly waits in the mornings with his boy at the end of the drive for the school bus. At first the dog tries to follow his boy and board the school bus but sharp words from an otherwise pleasant bus driver teaches the puppy not to try and to stay at the roadside as the bus drives away. After school Prince can be found faithfully sitting sentry at the end of the drive waiting for when the bus stops at the end of the driveway and Earl emerges through the school bus doors. Ella believes she can almost see a smile on the little dogs face at the safe return of his boy every day after school.

Ella is glad that her son has such a deeply devoted friend in his pet dog. She had of course wished there was money for expensive toys for her son's birthday. Always she wishes there could be more money so that her children would not have to go without or make due. This one time she knows in her heart that the gift she has given that was without cost is most definitely the best gift Earl could have gotten. Perhaps next year she will have money for the store bought things she knows he hopes for.

She would not know it then, but in the years to come the gift she gave her son on his seventh birthday, a puppy she got from the free classifieds, would buoy the child through very troubled waters. Darker days are over the horizon, darker than she could ever imagine as she watches her son and his dog playing fetch in the tall autumn grass. It will be this unbreakable bond that saves the little boy in many ways, and protects her child when she can not.

CHAPTER FOUR

LIKE MOST SUNDAY MORNINGS Earl gets up from his bed early. An internal clock urging him to open his eyes around five thirty and put the coffee on to brew. This day he tries to be very quiet in his kitchen, seeing that Ben is still dead to the world on the sofa, trying not to wake either of his guests with any unnecessary clatter as he bumbles around in the dark. He wonders if he should start the porridge but then decides to wait until everyone is out of bed. Still quiet, he washes up in the bathroom, finds his slippers, then pours himself a fresh hot cup of coffee. He adds a spoonful of sugar, and carries the hot drink outside to the chair on the step where he often sits to watch the morning sunrise.

It's an odd feeling knowing that there are other people inside. Earl has been alone most of his life, at least it has usually felt that way. Other than his beloved dog and an occasional overnight guest it has always been just Earl living under this roof. Just inside the door his world is changing. It's a good thing to help Ben and James, he knows this, but still he takes these changes a little uncomfortably. He is also awkward with the thought that there are likely many more disruptions and changes to come. Pleasant and invited changes are, after all, still changes. Change does not come easily to Earl.

The sun has just begun to ease over the horizon shedding it's golden rays of brightness across the green fields and wooded forests that span before his modest acreage. Earl's chair is a wooden rocker with faded and flaking brown paint. Next to his rocker is a small green plastic milk crate that serves as a small table, and two white wicker lawn chairs he had found discarded at the garbage dump two years past still in what he considers to be in good condition. Not there because he can't afford new chairs, just that he enjoys a good find. Perfectly usable after a hardy spray with a pressure washer so why leave them at the garbage dump?

The quiet of morning is one of his favourite times of day. He savours the peace and quiet of the awakening daylight hours as he settles into the old brown rocker and stretches his legs out. He takes a long sip of coffee and surveys the changing shades and shimmers of the green landscape before him. Mornings like this are always a time for peace and reflection before his day begins. He feels these peaceful morning moments are key to his inner strength and calm.

"Sir, why don't you have no cows or chickens?" James hollers, louder than he intends as he comes around the side of the house, startling Earl from that place of calm serenity.

It had been dark when they arrived in the night and the child awoke earlier anxious to explore his new home and surroundings. Ben had told James very little about his uncle except that Earl lived in the country. James has a picture book about the country so James was kind of expecting certain things. Things he imagined would be seen at a country home. He also recalls stories that his grandma Grace had shared about growing up in the country with farm animals and such.

"I'm not a farmer."

"You live in the country though?"

"Yep. Why you up so darn early?"

"Strange bed. Take time to settle I guess. No dog either, huh?"

"Nope."

"But you got a old dog house there?"

"Yup."

The boy squares his footing and stares. His intensity silently questioning his uncle Earl. He refrains from asking any more questions although it seems obvious that things here are really not quite what he had expected. Earl takes another slow sip from his coffee cup and stares back.

At length and without a spoken request the child assumes a seat in one of the weathered wicker chairs, the one closest to where Earl sits trying to relax with his coffee. James intently looks out at the green landscape before them. It seems to have a life of it's own, shifting and swaying beneath the rising sun as a morning breeze slides shadows of low lying clouds over the subtle dance of the far off fields. The landscape reveals new shades developing from near darkness from deep in the forests as the light of the dawning sun stretches across the woods and wheat fields in the valley. He had certainly not seen anything like this living in the city.

Earl pretends not to notice James' obvious mimicking gestures as the boy uncomfortably tries to stretch out his short legs while watching the building yellow orange brilliance of the early sun. James, like Earl, folds his arms against the morning chill until the sun's warm rays stretch gradually to the step to melt the chill away. When Earl is finished his first cup of coffee of the day he breaches the silence.

"Let's go in", he mumbles.

"What for sir?"

"I'll make us breakfast."

"Might as well, you got nothing out here." James whimpers with a mockery of sternness comical from a small six year old child. "You got no toys or dog or nothing to play with out here."

CHAPTER FIVE

"Thanks for breakfast Earl."

"Thank you sir." James chimes as he removes the dishes from the table.

"He always so helpful?"

"Mostly."

Earl reaches out and tousles the boys sandy blonde hair evoking a sigh of disapproval from the freckle faced child. James cocks his head away from his uncle Earl's big calloused mechanics hand.

"I'm not a baby Sir. I got hands for helping. That's what my Grandma would say."

"He's used to doing things for himself Earl. That, and he used to do lots of helping at Grace's house. His mom.............., well, he is very independent. Self sufficient."

"I see." Earl replies, "Kind of like me."

"Yeah sir, kinda like you." James pipes in.

"I can't thank you enough for helping us out and taking James in while I straighten out this mess I'm in. I really didn't know where else to turn." Ben struggles to hide the strain in his voice and suppresses an urge to spill his emotions. Not in front of the boy. Not in front of the man. Definitely not now when he is preparing to leave for the long drive back to the city. Not a good time to get all emotional and stirred up he thinks to himself.

"I'm gonna wash up then I'll have to hit the road." It's a stronger sounding statement than what he is feeling inside. Almost steadfast, without any hint that his life is in shambles. Ben has never been away from James for more than a day until now. He has recently lost his mother, doesn't know where his wife is at all, and is preparing to leave the most important thing in his world with his uncle Earl. Earl is practically unknown, a stranger to James, yet he is really the only person Ben can consider family and he is Ben's best option. Truth be told he'd be lying if he said there was any other options to consider.

"You guys will be fine together, right?"

"Don't worry about us Ben, you just take care of things at home. You can call us every night. We're already getting along good. Don't worry."

"Yeah dad, don't worry." The boy seems so brave, always strait-laced, not child-like. Traits developed out of necessity Ben guesses, and a need for self preservation. Ben is at least relieved that James and Earl seem to have warmed to each other. It will make his leaving here easier.

After a brief, and to the point farewell Ben drives away down the dirt road. Earl and James go back inside the house and Earl washes the breakfast dishes. Without Earl even having to ask him James pulls a chair to the cupboard to stand on and takes the dish towel in hand to dry the cups and plates.

"Thank you James, I usually leave 'em to air dry. Leaves time for other things."

"O.K. sir."

"You can call me Earl or uncle."

"O.K. Earl," He exposes a hint of a smile. "You can call me James."

"I ain't actually your uncle, not by blood. I was friends with your grandma Grace a long time ago. She took care of me like I'm to take care of you and I lived with her and your dad for a while like you are to live here with me, that's why your dad calls me uncle."

"You ain't nobody's uncle?"

"Sure, yeah, my brother Art has kids so that makes me their uncle. I don't see them much cause they don't live near here. Any matter, if we're gonna live together we best be like friends and call each other by name."

"O.K. Earl, I'll like you to be my friend." James doesn't let on that he is in short supply of friends. Back home there was grandma Grace, but then she went "to be with the angels" and James was left to be with his mother while his dad was at work.

James' mother was attentive and loving in his infant years but lately she would often leave him home alone while she went out, or worse bring her strange friends into their house after her husband Ben would leave for work. James didn't like his mothers strange new friends and would hide in his bedroom, usually in the closet with the lights out, and wait all day for his dad. Then last week she went out and never came back. James couldn't understand why she would do that. He had waited quietly alone all day.

His dad, Ben, stayed home with him a couple days after that and they went to the police station a lot. Ben was on the phone a lot too, whispered conversations not meant for James to hear. He didn't know how many days went by but then his dad told James he would have to go away and stay with gramma's friend Earl cause looking for his wife was becoming a full time job and otherwise he might also lose his real job, his paying work job. James tries to understand but like most things that are happening he doesn't really understand.

Ben tells James about the nice man named Earl, uncle Earl, who was good friends with his gramma Grace for a long time. James thought that would be alright. If gramma Grace liked this Earl guy then that means something. He missed his gramma a lot since the funeral. He misses his mom too, but not so much. Not in a similar way.

He never liked those lonely times and spending time with his mom was always lonely, lonely and sometimes scary. Nobody said it out right but he thought she must be very sick. She had needles and always pills to take. Her friends were sick too and had pills to take. They helped his mom with her needles and she helped them. James stayed in his room because he was scared of his mom's sick friends and also so he wouldn't get sick too.

There was preschool for a short time, other kids to play with, but that became a problem when his mother would forget to pick him up and his dad would have to leave his work to get him at the end of the school day. Sometimes he went back to his dad's work, but had to be quiet and still there too.

At preschool there were other kids and they could play and move and talk. The teacher was kind and pleasant and cheerful and the other kids were always fun to play with. James sort of missed them kids. A lot of fun things always happened at preschool, drawing and playing games with numbers and colours, but he never really got to know them kids and now that it was over he couldn't even remember one name.

Mostly he misses his gramma Grace. He furtively hopes that Earl will be more nice like his gramma was, and not scary or confusing like his mother. It was early to know for sure but so far he was happy here and now Earl says they can be friends and James feels that slight dark feeling lift from inside him a little bit. The change does not come comfortably to James but he thinks about the way things were before he came here and tells himself that changes will be good and he will be more comfortable here in time and he won't have to hide and be quiet any more. His dad had even said as much on the drive up from the city, that there would be a lot of changes. So far, James resolves, his dad sure was right.

CHAPTER SIX

"You like church James?"

"I don't know. What's church?"

"Oh!" Earl pauses, a little surprised. "It's a place I go on Sundays to hear about God and about God's work and some of my friends go there too." Earl chooses his words more carefully then because he doesn't want James to feel negatively for the experience like kids sometimes do. Earl had not been fond of church as a child when he was first taken there by his mother and step father.

"There's singing and stories like at school and there's other kids, kids like you, that go to church with their families. Then afterwards there is sandwiches and juice that the ladies make. I went to church sometimes with your gramma Grace when I was a kid."

"Kids?" James is hopeful, but also rather doubtful that the kids here are anything like him. "There was singing and stories at play school and I heard about God from my gramma. We never went to church together because I stay with dad on his day off from work and that was on gramma's church day but my gramma talked about church and God and I know He is in heaven with my gramma and his Jesus. And I know that Jesus was born for Christmas and got born again for Easter."

"Well then James you already know lots. The very first time I went to church I didn't even know that much."

The two take turns washing up in the bathroom, Earl shaves, and they both put on clean shirts. They go out to Earl's old Ford pick up truck to drive to the Sunday gathering at a little country church, Presbyterian, not far away.

James is little and can't reach the door handle of the truck or even climb to the high truck seat on his own. Earl lifts the boy up taking note of how thin and light he is. James then must scoot himself over across the seat rather quickly to avoid being hit by the closing door. Earl shuts it firmly and walks around to the drivers side to get in the truck himself.

"Earl?" James asks, trying out the name and wondering if he will more comfortable saying Uncle or Earl, as Earl starts his truck, "are you gonna do up my seat belt for me? I ain't safe if you don't."

Earl reaches over and fastens the boy in place. Lots to remember with a kid in tow he tells himself. He wonders if the child has buttoned his shirt and pants correctly and if there is dirt behind his ears or under his fingernails. He glances over at the child and a quick scan reveals that nothing is unbuttoned or out of place. Earl is relieved but wonders to himself about the care and maintenance of a child.

As he drives down the country road that will lead to the little church Earl thinks about another time at church when he was a child. A long time ago when he was small and thin and light and knew so little about church. A day that he would never forget.

CHAPTER SEVEN

"Mamma, are we gonna have to move to a new house?"

Earl is unsure about a lot of things going on in his life, many changes are coming, about that he has no control. His mom is getting married. The man, his name is Harold, makes Earl tense but Earl tries to hide it because his mom says she is super happy because she isn't lonely anymore. Also she has explained that Harold has a job so they wont have to "make due" no more. Earl isn't sure why his mother should be lonely, she has him and Prince around all the time. Earl never feels lonely with her and Prince. On the other hand he has never had to not "make due" and that sounds like it will be nice.

"No Earl, Harold will come live with us in our house and we'll all be a family. You will have the same room, and the same friends, and the same school bus driver." It sounds alright but Earl feels a knot building in his stomach. "Now let's get your tie straightened, and don't slouch. You know Harold doesn't like it when you slouch."

Earl wants to say that Harold doesn't like much of anything but he doesn't want to make his mom upset. He wishes he could ask his big brother what to do, but Art has already come and gone.

"Is Art gonna be there mom?"

"No Earl, Art had other things to do. He had to leave."

"Is he coming back?" Earl had heard his mom and brother argue earlier. They were yelling about Harold and Art made their mother cry. Earl didn't want to see his mom cry no more cause she said it was gonna be a real happy day.

"Is he coming back mom?"

"Oh there's the music, now stand up straight and don't fidget. Harold doesn't like it when you fidget."

She never answers the question about Art and although he didn't want Art to make their mom cry no more Earl isn't glad that Art had to leave and is not coming back. In fact the knot in his stomach seems to tighten just a little more. He wishes Prince could be there with him but Harold says no dogs at the wedding. Harold has lots of rules like that.

Harold's rules are all rules that Earl doesn't like much, but his mom keeps saying she is so happy, that Harold makes her so happy and buys her things and is gonna take care of them and they won't have to rely on government assistance and "make due" so Earl decides he will try his very best to be good and follow all the new rules that Harold makes. He will at least try for his mom. He loves his mom and thinks she should be happy. She says they will all be happy after today. There will be some changes because weddings change things but she says things are gonna change for the better.

After a very private wedding in the empty church where all their voices echo they go out to a Chinese restaurant for a nice supper, just the three of them. Harold orders for everyone. Earl's blue suit is itchy and uncomfortable and the shirt and tie are tight at the collar. He tries not to, but Earl squirms and fidgets the whole time. The food is strange and Earl does not care for it but he cleans his plate as his mom and Harold watch. He can feel his newly acquired step father glare unpleasantly at him and is glad when the whole ordeal is over because that means he is getting to stay at Frank's house overnight for two nights.

Frank's parents are nice, they even let him bring Prince for the sleepover. Frank says having a mom and a dad is way better than just a mom so Earl tries to be positive. Earl does not remember his own dad but Frank says having a dad is really good. Still these changes are strange and uncomfortable. He tries to ignore those gut feelings because everyone seems to be saying that the changes happening are good changes. Everyone except Earl and Art.

After the sleepover it is Harold, not Ella, who picks Earl and Prince up at Frank's house and drives them home. When they get back home it is to something quite different. There are some different furnishings that Earl guesses belong to Harold, and the living room has been rearranged to fit some of the new things in. Earl's mom looks a little different to him, and although he doesn't understand what has changed he knows that things are different now. Something inside tells him not to ask too many questions. This not asking questions is very difficult for a boy Earl's age.

"You've never had a man around Earl so I'll explain how things are going to be now," Harold begins as they unpack Earl's overnight bag. "I'm the man of the house now. The man makes all the rules. Rule number one is respect. There are lots of ways for you to show your respect. I will teach you. You have a lot to learn."

There are rules for meal time and bed time and quiet time and work time. There is no mention of play time. There will be chores in the morning and silence at night and church on Sunday. At Harold's church they wear black suits and dresses, never blue suits or anything that isn't black. There is a time for everything and the time is known to Harold and so Harold will tell Earl what he should do and what time to do it.

Earl is tense and scared as he puts his clothing and toys away, probably for the first time that he can ever remember. He feels it through and through without having any understanding why except the authoritative tone in Harold's voice as he lists too many rules for Earl to remember. Earl is scared for himself and for his mom without having any notion of why he feels that way, like someone else's voice is telling his head to be careful because the changes might not be safe. There are moments that it feels like Harold might have control of the whole world, and the power to block out the sun. Earl feels a cold chill as he listens to all of Harold's rules and instructions on how to respect him, and he desperately tries not to fidget. He tries to remember the rules and what Frank said about having a dad and what his mom said about being happy and he pushes away his fears for the new and changing future with Harold in their lives.

CHAPTER EIGHT

"Sometime church gets a bit long James, are you a fidgety type?"

"Oh no, I'm real good at being quiet." James shares with a hinted sense of pride for mastering this skill so well. "I hope I don't fall asleep. I do that sometimes when the waiting gets long. Is that what you mean?"

"I'll nudge you if I see you nodding off." Earl offers.

Earl gets the sense that James has had more than his fair share of waiting and trying to be quiet. Ben has told him about his wife's drug abuse and how she couldn't be trusted, not even with her own son. Earl wonders, maybe Ben has held back some of those less than comfortable and scary details. More likely, Earl imagines, James has held back and that the child has come from a place where he is not permitted to fidget and where every day is a day of waiting without knowing what he is waiting for. Earl can strongly identify with that.

When they arrive at the church and go inside it is warm and inviting inside. There are three long white candles burning on a beautifully carved wooden table at the front of the church. A thin man with grey hair and thick eyeglasses plays the piano to the right of the table, and in the center there is a pulpit for standing at draped with a fancy cloth. Red with gold trim. The people who are already seated in rows and scattered sparsely around the big room smile and nod in acknowledgement to Earl as he walks in but nobody calls out. It is real quiet and peaceful, even the piano music is soft and calm.

There are a few other kids there like Earl said there would be. They point straight at James and whisper to their parents. James instinctively reaches up for Earl's hand and steps a little closer. A blush of shyness reddens his neck and he feels very small, smaller than usual, and unsure in this strange place with so many strange faces.

Earl chooses a place for them in the second last pew on the left. James is relieved to be close to the door, and sits very close to Earl. The faded denim of the leg of his Jeans leg brushing against Earl's as his short legs dangle over the edge of the smooth dark wooden bench. He seems to Earl to be an entirely different boy than the intrepid young explorer from earlier this morning.

"Do you know all these people uncle Earl?" James whispered without knowing why he should feel the need to whisper.

"Most. I don't know them all, but they all come to share the word of God, just like us. There used to be more but it seem to get less every year."

"Do I have to share? I didn't bring nothing to share."

"Sometimes nothing is still something. We're here and that's all God asks."

James doesn't know what Earl means and he never heard anyone asking them anything but then this whole thing is confusing to him. Why do they all have to get together to share about God? Why not just pick up the phone and say "Hey neighbour, I know something about God"? Why couldn't they just have stayed home and talked about God there?

A few more people arrive and the an older grey haired man in a black robe and a red scarf that matches the cloth on the pulpit comes out from behind a door in the corner that James had not noticed before. All the people get quiet and turn to the front to listen to the man.

"God be with you." He announces cheerfully with a broad smile and outstretched arms.

"And also with you." All the people responded in unison.

James sits and listens as the man in the robe tells a story about Jesus sharing his bread and fish with all the people who were hungry. Then James stands beside Earl as everybody rises to their feet to sing a church song. Then they sit and pray with their heads bowed and their hands folded. Then the man talks some more about Jesus and the importance of giving and how giving makes your heart cheerful. Next beautiful wooden plates get passed around from one person to the next and then on to the next row, one for each side of the church, and everybody shares a little money into the plates. Then more singing, more talking, more praying, then it is over. James didn't fall asleep at all the whole time and he is very glad.

Next the preacher strolls down the centre of the church and then outside and stops to stand on the step. Then everyone follows and shake his hand as they walk out the building, the other children run around together but James stays with Earl. It all seems rather peculiar to James. Earl and James, having sat at the back, are among the last to leave the building. Outside the sun has risen warm and bright in the midday sky.

James had relaxed some and even enjoyed the service song selections, Earl called them Hymns. That relaxed feeling is leaving him now and he once again holds tight to Earl's big hand and keeps very quiet as all those other church people walk past them and look down at him. As they are also leaving the secure comforts of the church to step outside into the gathered crowd a pretty lady approaches.

"Hey Earl, is this the young man your were telling me about? The one who will be staying with you?'

"This is James."

"Hi." The lady says to them but she's looking at Earl. Then she bends down to be eye level, "Hi James." softer now. "My name is Amber." She has nice yellow hair and friendly white teeth. He remembers that Amber is the one who had baked the chocolate cake they had enjoyed the night before.

"Hi." it comes out, a barely audible trace of his voice. James opens his mouth to repeat, but his mouth is dry. Small finger grip Earl's larger ones a bit tighter as James slinks behind a denim clad leg.

"Earl," She sweetly scolds, "This boy is terribly parched. Come on inside and let's get a juice for him."

Back inside the little country church Amber pours orange juice into a white paper cup and hands it to James. Earl gets himself a coffee. Releasing his fingers from James' tightened grip he takes two napkins and two egg salad sandwiches before motioning the boy to sit with him back in the pew they had shared earlier. Other ladies have come inside with trays of sandwiches and squares and now busy themselves around the food table at the back of the church as the church parishioners return inside for food and visiting. Amber joins Earl and James with a sandwich and a hot coffee of her own.

James is glad to have something to nibble on knowing he won't be asked to talk to anyone with a mouthful of sandwich. He is very careful not to drop any crumbs or spill his juice, he tries very hard to be good and quiet. He listens as Earl and Amber talk back and forth. They make plans to have dinner at Amber's house. She mentions that her dog Lucy has six puppies. This is something interesting for James but still he stays quiet. They talk about Earl's work schedule. James is aware that all of these things have impact on him, still he stays quiet, staring up at the church's stained glass windows and saying nothing even after his sandwich is gone.

Amber leaves them to visit with others and a bearded man comes over to greet Earl, a man Earl introduces as his hunting buddy and good friend Gerald. They talk about truck parts and their last quading trip and the upcoming hunting season. James doesn't know what most of that is so he stays quiet some more.

There are strange faces, indiscreet eyes glancing in his direction. Unfamiliar talk about things he doesn't understand in a place that is completely foreign to him and where everyone is oddly happy and they sing songs called "God Loves a Cheerful Giver". All James can think is how he wishes he could disappear, like in his bedroom closet back at home. Then he reprimands himself for being homesick like that. Subconsciously he fidgets, tearing his paper cup to tiny pieces.

"I think we ought to head out. What do you say James." Earl asks his now completely muted companion.

A nod is all he can muster as he gathers the remnants of his cup.

Earl holds out a big flat hand. James fills it with the paper bits of his cup. Earl stuffs them in his jeans pocket.

Earl again reaches out this time taking the boy's hand in his. The relief James feels is almost dizzying as they leave the church and Earl puts him up in the truck and fastens his seatbelt. James' shy detachment puzzles Earl as he closes the door and walks around to the drivers side of the vehicle. He thought that James would like church but James appears very sad. "What thoughts are churning under this boy's calm exterior?" he wonders but he does not immediately press the child with questions.

Driving away from the church he is about to say something when James begins an impromptu ramble.

"My mom took me out to the mall sometimes. There is a food court at the mall where people buy sandwiches and drinks and mom would meet her friends there and they would tell stories." James begins his unexpected chatter. "There was sleepy music and lots of people that I didn't know and some of them looked smooth and pretty like plastic. They wear bright clothing, lots of people in bright clothing, and talk extra loud." There's a brief pause for breath, then he continues.

"Sometimes Santa Clause was supposed to be there but I never saw Santa Clause, and not the Easter bunny either. I saw a big picture of Santa and just a lot of people. Some just go and sit or eat and some buy stuff in stores and they all talk a lot so you can't hardly hear the sleepy music. Mom and her friends were loud like that. Everything was loud except the sleepy music, but I liked the music."

"Doesn't sound too much like church people." Earl responds.

"No," James confirms, "Mall people aren't much like church people."

James continues, winding up his story. "Not much at all. I like the church people."

CHAPTER NINE

MOST OF HAROLD'S RULES don't make any sense to Earl. He may not eat dinner at the dinner table until Harold is done and finished and has removed himself away from the table. He may not have his friend Frank over because Harold doesn't like Frank's dad. He may not watch T.V. unless Harold approves the program and has time to watch it with him. He may not speak unless spoken to. Sometimes Earl tries to argue the feasibility of these points but Harold grabs his shoulders and squeezes so hard it brings tears to Earl eyes and leaves red bruises on his pink skin.

Earl's mother pulls him aside and pleads with him to try to do what Harold wants. She promises that things will get better once Harold is settled in and more comfortable. She promises the rules would not apply when Harold is at work and it is just the two of them. She tells Earl she will try to change Harold's mind on some of those rules, but it will take time and they will have to be patient. She says the changes are difficult for Harold too, that they must all make sacrifices, even Harold. And so Earl, who had been until now used to being in charge of himself and how he spends his time, haltingly relinquishes his all of his freedom to Harold. That is, until bedtime.

"That dog ain't sleeping inside this house, animals don't sleep under the same roof as people. This ain't no barn it's a house. Not under my roof. People are better than animals and dogs are useless. They don't produce anything or offer any value." Harold proclaims. "That mutt sleeps outside. It ain't people, it ain't family, it's just a damn mutt."

"He's not a mutt. He's a real dog with a name that I gave him. His name is Prince and Prince sleeps with me." Earl counters. "Always has."

"Harold, please, can't the boy have his dog?" Ella defends, but an icy cold glare from Harold mutes her in the middle of her words.

"The dog sleeps outside! Did you NOT hear me the first time?" Harold's voice booms loud and static. It isn't really a question, Harold despises having to repeat himself and a visible red rage is now brewing behind his cold eyes.

"Prince sleeps with me!" Earl defiantly counters again. "He don't know how to sleep outside by his self, he ain't never done that in his whole life."

The man menaces a step towards the child. Earl's eight year old frame is small, and his eyes well with angry tears but he squares his shoulders bracing for an argument that he fully intends to win. What comes instead is the solid flat palm of Harold's hand hard to his jaw. Earl, falling to the floor, catches a glimpse of Prince's furry brown body leaping in Earl's defence towards Harold and then his mom seizing the dog in mid-air before falling to the floor at her angry husband's feet.

"Please Harold," she begs "Please." Child and pet behind her in the corner of the kitchen, she has to think fast. "What about a compromise, just this once, just for this. I'll make it up to you..... . I'll do anything you want, anything, just let the dog stay inside. Please Harold," She urgently pleads. "I'll do anything you like. Just a small compromise, please."

Ella hopes she appears strong for Earl's sake, but she feels utterly deflated and fearful cowering before the intimidating man. She wants to be strong for Earl. She is now desperately torn between her husband and her son. It doesn't even occur to her to put the dog out and end the dispute, in her heart the dog is family. There on the floor protecting her family she believes at that moment that her once happy life may be completely lost and invisible and the compromises to come will be made by her and by Earl, and not by Harold. In that moment she wants to please everyone in the room; her husband, her son, even the dog.

She can feel the tables turning and knows then, in that very instant, that things might never turn back. She wants to tell herself she will regain some leverage when Harold has had time to cool off. She doesn't recognize this raving man as the person she came to love and recently married, the man she has vowed to love and obey. She sees the unbroken gold band on Harold's ring finger and glances down at her own trembling hand.

Harold is a new and monstrous stranger dark with rage to whom she is wed, and that fact is now shocking and scary to her. Even more frightening is the realization that she doesn't recognize herself at this moment either. Harold is changing before her very eyes and she sees with deafening clarity how that changes everything including herself. Ella thinks then of her sons, both Earl and Art, and she feels a churning sickness inside herself. How could she have not seen this?

Maybe it will just take time, time and patience with her new husband and for now she will just have to think of little compromises. Just to get through this night, just this one time, she would let him win without a fight. Just one small compromise.

"Can't Prince sleep in the porch or the basement? Please Harold."

Harold's ugly fierceness lessens, but the blaze of his eyes does not dim.

"Basement, O.K., the basement." he snarls from his curled lips as a deep consuming breath fills his lungs and expands his chest as it empties the air around her. "And you owe me for that." This concession will not be without reprisal or a price. He defines it, she sees it coming, and the child is only vaguely understanding the meaning and the price of his mother's small compromise. His concern in this moment is still for his dog, his best friend.

Earl is sent straight to his room, to bed then, without even a hug or kiss from his mom. Fear and loneliness fill the darkening corners as he lays there beneath his Ninja Turtle blanket. He can not possibly sleep this way, so he waits. He waits for his mom and Harold to stop yelling, catching only pieces of the conversation, but hearing with dread when Harold proclaims he will leave his job if he must until he can gain control of his home and his family. Earl feels a deepening dread as he listens to their argument and worsening fear as the house grows quiet, still, and dark.

Earl remains still, waiting for the clock to chime more than ten and the house to be muted in uncertainties, but it is not still. He can hear his best friend whimpering far below in the basement. Then in the darkness, as discrete as possible, he gathers his pillow and blankets and makes his way down the dark stairs feeling his hand against the walls.

Shadows dance from the swinging light at the base of the narrow basement stairwell, dim and haunting. Earl tells himself to be brave. The wood burning furnace crackles from within and an orange glow flickers in the cracks around it's steal door. The wood pile looms in the corner stacked against the cinder block walls and wind sighs through the hatch in the wall where they put the fire wood through from the outside. Heavy planks cover most of the dirt floor, but Earl can smell the dirt and the wood and the heat.

Prince whimpers softly in the darkness and Earl finds him and comforts him with hugs and kisses. He spreads his blanket down on the floor and then nestles in with Prince for some much needed sleep.

The change for Earl; he feels like he will always be holding his breath from here on out, and in that moment like he will never again exhale and breath and he knows that there are many breathless days to come. Distant lights seemed brighter then, and the air is so white he can not see through it. Edges grow sharper, every thought cutting deeper than the last. Sad green eyes flood with tears and shine in the darkness as he holds his dog tightly. He imagines himself a timid spaceman walking on the surface of the sun. He will from this time forward suffer fright and surprise at every outburst and flare expected or not, and all the while he will be engulfed in Harold's heated temper with no real place of refuge.

Prince snuggles his soft body against Earl bringing him back to the reality of his present surroundings. He will do anything for his pet, his best friend, even sleep in the basement to protect him. Together in the dark farm house basement, with the smells of wood and fire and dirt, they close their eyes and sleep. Earl is glad to be together with Prince but is wondering about his mother and if she is crying too.

CHAPTER TEN

"Do you wanna tell me what you're feeling?" Earl asks as he drives his Ford truck down the gravelled lane.

"I ain't used to so many people Uncle, but I liked the singing."

They are quiet then. Earl assuming a need for delicacy. James feeling like Earl is waiting for something more from him. Maybe it's just that he himself has more to say. He has a deep feeling of discomfort with all this talking about feelings but he soldiers on.

"Can I just call you uncle?"

"Whatever suits you best, I'd be fine with that." Earl smiles in his answer as he brings the truck to a stop in front of Amber's house.

"Will there be other people here uncle?"

"No just you and me and Amber, she has a son, David, he lives in town. He's nice like Amber, you'll see. You might meet him later, another day, but not today. Today it'll just be us."

Earl reaches over and unbuckles James' seatbelt, then he gives the boy's hand a tender squeeze. "I've never been much for people either, just at church. Mostly I just like the singing too."

"The windows are sure nice. I never seen so many colours. That church sure has pretty windows uncle."

"I think so too, it's called stained glass. Lots of churches have stained glass. They are nice in the day time, but you should see that little church at night when everything is dark on the outside and the light from the inside shines through, that is a remarkable sight to see. When you see it shining from the inside out you will think that little old church is the most

38

beautiful church in the world. At least that is what I think. I'm glad you like it James. We can go together again and I wouldn't be going alone no more. I would like that."

CHAPTER ELEVEN

EARL REALIZES QUICKLY THAT he has changed the course of life as he knows it by choosing to sleep in the basement to protect his dog on that first night. Still, he feels a deep foreboding fear that Harold would hurt Prince, really hurt him, or even take him away if he was not right there at every moment to protect his pet. He can only recognize afterwards that Harold views his act of defiance as an admission of surrender. His surrender to the basement.

Ella tries to get Earl to sleep in his bedroom on following nights but stubbornly Earl will not bend or abandon his pet. Harold's growing control over them is wretchedly reinforced by Earl's rebellion to his rules. That night, and every night after for a very long time, Earl sleeps in the basement with his dog Prince. His only compromise, the only way Earl will return to his room, will be if Prince and he can return to the comforts of the bedroom together. Without compromise Harold refuses, sometimes violently, to entertain the idea. Harold does not make compromises.

At some point, it seems like weeks down the line, Earl's routine changes from enjoying his meals at the dinner table with his mother nearby to eating in the porch or the basement with only his dog Prince for company. He no longer waits until after Harold has gotten his fill, now he waits for scraps after the dishes are cleared. Sometimes he waits until dark when Harold and his mother are turning out the lights to go to bed. On these days Earl and Prince eat in the dark unsure of what the meal had been, only that even these cold chewy scraps are enough to fill their hunger. Eventually Earl loses the privilege of utensils as well. Harold's reasoning for this rule has something to do with Earl's choice to live with the dog like an animal. Ella tries in vain to argue, Earl also resists. It take very little time until they eventually bend to Harold's newest demands, they both bear the bruises of proof for the consequences of non-compliance to Harold's authority.

Earl can't separate in his mind if this new shift in himself is born out of fear or pride or protectiveness of the dog. He simply and stubbornly accepts this seemingly natural condemnation as yet another unpleasant change in his life. Harold talks circles around him until all of Harold's rules and reasoning have their own warped and twisted logic. At first Earl does not wholeheartedly mind the changes. It seems better to eat with his best friend in the veils of darkness in the basements than stiffly seated in the glaring brightness of the kitchen under Harold's disapproving glare.

The next humiliation comes when Earl tries to sneak Prince into the bathroom for a shared bath like they would have done in the old days. Just a boy and his dog having a tub. Living in the filth of a dusty basement is a foul living, even to a boy of eight and his dog. He sneaks because even though Harold has not said is would be breaking an unspoken rule Earl just knows that Harold would not ever approve.

The punishment for getting into Harold's clean bath tub with this filthy dog, Harold's newest rule, Earl loses the privilege of having hot water drawn for his bath, only cold. Harold's rule; dogs, and boys who choose to live like dogs are not welcome to enjoy the same luxuries as the people do. The people being Harold and Ella, sometimes not even Ella. Yet "cold" does not begin to describe the feeling. The freezing bath is almost unbearable for Earl, a cold that draws the breath right out of his lungs and creates an instant ache in his head and chest. The demeaning portion of this is surpassed only by the actual physical pain of the icy bath water that cuts sharp into his young flesh.

Earl soon prefers no bath at all to this new chilling horror. He tries to resist, and yet it becomes a weekly ritual supervised by Harold himself. Earl is stubborn; rebels at first, takes some hard slaps, then gives in. His safety is with Prince and if he must eat table scraps in the dark basement and live a life without hot water baths as his declaration of independence, he will do just that and he will do it without surrender. At the time, for a boy his age, some of these compromises seem not so bad. Earl is increasingly defiant telling himself not to bend and that Harold will under no circumstances win this war. At least there is some small comfort to tell himself things are not so bad and to stand firm without giving in. Blindly, through his very stubborn defiance Earl eventually succumbs to each and every one of Harold's demands.

Earl notices changes in his mom also. She becomes thinner over time. Really skinny, and quiet too. Not all at once. Like Earl her changes are gradual. Her hair gets dull, then her skin, then her eyes too. She smiles less and less, then not at all. At the beginning she fights her husband, but he wears down her spirits. He wears her down day after day and eventually she relinquishes all her hopes. She loses the glowing light of confidence to dull surrender. She stops defending the dog, stops defending her son, stops defending herself. Harold is like a burning heat and everything around him begins to wither. This is especially true for Ella.

Ella works relentlessly to try to keep her husband happy. Subserviently she cleans all day, the house and herself, but is insecure and mumbles to herself about how it is never good enough and how she is not trying hard enough. Her friends telephone sometimes but she does not even bother any effort to pick up the phone, she know these things have their price. Eventually friends call to visit less and less, then not at all.

Ella cries in the night. She sleeps in the day. Her child sees all the things that she tries to hide. Burns and bruises. Her once cheerful eyes lost in shallow wells of grey.

When Ella believes her son Earl isn't near to see her she eats the antidepressant pills that she keeps hidden in the bathroom and drinks Harold's alcohol straight from the bottle. Sadly these habits are no remedy for her pain. These stolen liberties are always met with dire consequences. Earl can hear her cries in the deathly stillness of the house just as he can feel her sobs to the core of his spine as if they were his own. Death is happening to them, to Earl, to Ella, to the house itself. It is a gradual succumbing to multiplying losses as every day Harold takes greater gains.

On the outside Ella becomes as tranquil as death itself, inside she is a delicately fabricated mountain of fears and secrets. In vain she attempts to obey her husbands many commands and multiplying rules. Her life is eventually separated into two parts; there is the presence of Harold and in his absence there is the threat of Harold. She exposes occasional acts of defiance when Harold is on an outing or she thinks he isn't watching her; sneaking bits of food to Earl. Food that Earl always shares with his dearest friend Prince.

The entrenched monotony of a life lived without choices is frequently punctuated with upheaval. Marie and Frank stopping by unannounced are usually turned away by Harold. He makes his excuses, says that they are sick and not receiving visitors. Once or twice he allows Marie in for one cup of tea; he does not leave the room during these brief visits, presiding over the intrusion like a totalitarian overlord. Marie appears to want to help but seems to be waiting for Ella to ask her. Ella lives in constant fear and out of fear says nothing, asks for nothing, reveals nothing, pretends comfort she no longer has.

Twice that first summer Grace comes in her red Dodge car with her little brother Frank. They succeed in sneaking Earl away by parking at the road behind the trees and apprehending Earl through the bushes like furtive spies on a secret mission. On these blessed days they go to a nearby park, eat hot dogs, and play in the playground. Earl, although wanting to enjoy these escapes with his friends, is unable to relax and worries constantly about the safety of his mom and his dog left behind under Harold's menacing weight.

One day, mid September a concerned teacher from the school telephones to ask about Earl's whereabouts. Harold is home to take the call.

"Oh, hello Miss Price. I didn't realize you were still expecting Earl in your little school. I guess we have his mother to thank for that. The woman forgets everything." His tone is icy and condescending.

"We have decided to place little Earl in a special school." An out right lie if there ever was one. "You know how slow he is, two years of first grade with your public system and the boy still doesn't know his alphabet." There isn't really a new school.

"But we haven't had a transfer request ..... ."

"Look Miss Price, I'm sure you tried your best but Earl requires special help. He's what you in the system call Special Needs. Isn't that how you talk about children like Earl? He's much better off where he is at. It's not like you had any success trying to teach him with your ways. I'm sure you do fine with average children who aren't too challenging for a gal like you, but Earl isn't exactly average. I think it is fair to say that you'd be out of your league with instructing a child such as Earl."

"I'm sorry to have bothered you sir. Earl is an endearing boy, we here at the school are just concerned for his education."

"Well Miss Price, it's not really any concern of yours anymore is it?" His voice is harsh and dismissive and the conversation ends abruptly as he hangs up the receiver.

After that life for Earl becomes stagnant and days blend into weeks without change. Weeks blur into months. Earl forgets the things he knew in a life now lost and is content to just look at the pictures in books he had once yearned to read with his mother. There is no more need for math lessons or drawing or even play time. They fall into sameness and obscurity without waver, and no-one, not even Art, seems to miss them or call. Not that they would have known. One of Harold's newest rules is that only Harold may answer the telephone.

Earl loses his childlike hopefulness then. There is no reason to hope, only things to do to keep himself busy. He tries to help his mom with the outside chores, anything to affirm a feeling of value and worth. Earl does whatever he can, he watches to know the things his mother struggles with and those are the things he tries to do. His only thoughts become to help his mom in anyway that he can to keep Harold's rules appeased.

He becomes furtive and evasive in his actions, almost shadowlike, so that Harold might never know his whereabouts. It doesn't even once occur to him that the man just doesn't care as long as he and the dog are out of Harold's sight. When they are in Harold's sight Harold's angry outbursts seem to intensify. Ella and Earl's isolation builds until all they have is fear and each other. As they lose their daily battles even that seems lost.

Earl becomes adept at keeping the fire burning in the furnace at night as Autumn gradually turns into Winter, heaving heavy lengths of wood in to the smoky flames. He cleans the porch and even Harold's muddy boots. He gathers eggs from the hen house and sometimes boldly steals one or two for he and Prince. He develops his own routine of tasks to keep himself busy. Little tasks that would, in small ways help his mom, thus pleasing Harold. If Earl can please Harold in these ways he can then sometimes defer the man's angry tirades.

Although most of Earl's life is lived in a gloomy basement he is not blind to veiled abuses against his mother when Harold's rules and obscure wants are not satisfied. Earl even comes to believe it is sometimes worth the effort to occasionally act out and take the brunt of whatever horrible punishments Harold feels fit to inflict if it can distract the terrible man from spending his anger on Earl's mom, Ella. Harold is almost always angry. Gradually their daily life becomes as dark as their deepest bruises but still they survive. There is nothing here to do but to please this increasingly ominous man and thus survive, and every day becomes slow and gradual like a fading bruise. As has always been their way Earl and Ella settle in, adapt, and learn to "make due".

Somewhere along the line Earl realizes that his brother Art is not coming back, and who could blame him? Art will not be rescuing them, and it is all up to him. Earl feels fully responsible then for the family's safe keeping; for himself, his mom, and his dog. Everything he had dreamed in a former lifetime fades and is lost in a haze as a childhood and a child's spirit disappear.

Sometimes in the mornings Earl unlocks the front door and he and Prince slip outside before Harold or Ella are awake. He sits with Prince on the front step and shares a crust of bread or Earl sneaks a piece of over ripe fruit from the kitchen scraps that is meant for the hens in the barn yard.

Mornings are the best time of day, it is peaceful and quiet. Just Earl and Prince watching as the dark peacefulness of night dissolves into raging day and sunlight spreads across the farm yard. As the sunlight builds filling the morning skies Earl sometimes stares directly at the bright burning ball until it blinds his sight and his of his dismal existence is replaced by the blinding sun spots that burn at his retina. It is not better than the forgotten gray farmyard that surround him, it is just that the brightness strips everything else away.

He imagines again that he is trapped on the burning surface of the sun. it is not better, just far away from here. He longs desperately to be away from Harold and the rules, and the punishment. There on the wooden step Earl is almost able to dare himself to imagine some better life.

CHAPTER TWELVE

"Uncle?" James' question is a barely audible whisper in the truck on the way home from dinner at Amber's house Sunday evening, "Why did my mother stop loving me and daddy?"

He had listened closely and quietly over dinner to Earl explaining his situation to Amber. Maybe... , James is wondering, maybe Earl can tell him what he did wrong.

Earl slows the truck and stops on the shoulder of the road. He knows full well what the boy must be feeling but has no idea how to relieve these insecurities. "If only Grace were here" Earl dwells, "She would know exactly what to say". He has to swallow hard before he answers the child's question.

"James" he begins gently, "I want you to listen. Please listen careful to what I tell you........ ." He looks squarely at James, waits for a mute little nod, then continues. "Your mother never stopped loving you. She's stopped showing it, but be certain she still loves you."

"But what did I do wrong?" A single tear shimmers on his cheek.

"You haven't done nothing wrong. James you can be certain that you have never did nothing wrong." Earl reaches softly for the little boys hand, holds it lightly while he talks. "I'm sure that your mother did not stop loving you. Maybe she stopped showing it to you, but you are always in her heart. Mother's don't ever stop loving their son's. It's kind of like being lost and all alone and they don't know how to be warm cause they just get cold. Like a light goes out. Do you understand?"

"I don't," he struggles, "not really. I ain't never been lost. I don't understand, not at all. Why did she get cold and lost? I tried to be good. I really tried. I was quiet and good and I didn't do nothing bad. I really, really tried." A tear… a trickle… a stream now. "Can we fix her? Can we fix her light?"

"We will just have to be patient. We have to wait, and maybe she'll find her way, maybe her light can still shine again. She has to really try, it will be hard for her. She might stay lost a while. It's hard to find your way when your lost. It's like everything is dark and there's no light to guide you and not even any shadow. We just have to wait and see."

Earl releases his hold on James' small hands and unlatches the boy's seatbelt. James hesitates a moment. Earl then slides him closer, the middle of the truck's bench seat, fastens the center seatbelt across James' lap and places his arm around the disheartened boy. James softens…, leans…, crumples…., resting his weary head against Earl's ribs.

As Earl drives home he wonders if he has said the right things and what more he should do. Should he tell Ben about his son's questions and worries? Should he tell Ben about this conversation? Would he be telling Ben anything he didn't already know?

When Earl arrives home the sun is disappearing and the child is deeply sleeping. What Earl had hoped would be a bright and cheerful day ends in dark multiplying questions. James is weightless in Earl's arms as he is carried from the truck to the lamp lit house, changed into his pyjamas, and tucked into bed beneath warm Bat Man covers.

Standing in the kitchen Earl twists the cap from a beer bottle anticipating it's cool, wet, bitter taste but is interrupted by the chime of the telephone. He hastens to answer, not wanting the annoyance of the loud ringing to echo through the quiet house to wake the sleeping child in the next room.

"Hello."

"Earl, Ben here."

"The boy is sleeping."

"Calling to talk to you. I got fresh troubles."

"Go on." Phone to his ear, he swallows a mouthful from the beer bottle in his other hand.

"She's in the hospital. Someone found her beaten up in an alley off

Beacon Street. She's not conscious. I don't even recognize her. It's a blessing that James is there with you and not here."

"What should I tell him? What are the doctors saying?"

"I don't even know what to tell myself. They say she's critical. Don't tell him that. She's his mother, she's my wife, I wish I gave a damn but I genuinely don't know how anymore. I'm all tapped out. Just tell him what you think is best, you know, just enough so he understands."

"He's had a really rough day ......, hard shift." There is a long pause in the conversation.

"More than just the day Earl. I don't remember when it hasn't been hard for him this whole year. It was so hard for him to lose his gramma. This makes me so damn angry and I don't want it to do that to him too. How do you tell a child this kind of stuff? How can he possibly understand?"

"Don't know that he's up to it Ben. Don't worry about us though, I'll be gentle. You best get through the night and see what tomorrow brings."

"Thanks. Thanks for everything, I mean that. I'll call again tomorrow. Seems all we can do now is wait."

Earl hangs up the receiver. Bens words, "all we can do is wait" hanging heavy like a Winter ice fog. For Earl there is something about waiting that always feels like the end. Beer in one hand, throw from the sofa in the other, he shuffles to the front door and then out.

As the blue sky fades to black the moon is a sliver of coldness in the warm night sky. Warm, but soon enough the Autumn winds will chill the air. Multitudes of delicate stars glitter the atmosphere, more still flicker beneath a shift of scattering cloudy wisps. The Summer air is promising, the breeze glides through like the reverent touch of a blind man. This is the peace Earl knows best.

Earl slumps into the familiar curve of the creaky old rocker on the step, it is the place he prefers to start and end each day. A peaceful place where he does not need to think. There is a comfortable layer of shades and shadows as more stars emerge in the blue black heavens. Sipping his beer, the day slip away but still tomorrows troubles creep upon him like an early frost. Question without answers tumble through his thoughts. Tomorrow seems stark and without promise.

Earl gathers his beer bottle and blanket and returns to the comforts of the living room. He telephones his boss to take the following day off from work, then turns on the evening news on the television. World events serve as no distraction to the rapidly changing upheavals he has invited into his previously placid life. He wonders about James, where the child would be if he were not here with him. The beer empties quickly, as does the next. He dwells momentarily on past life trauma. Dwells longer on James' words and how they echoed his own childhood fears. Where would he be today if things were different in his own tumultuous childhood? Where would he be if Grace had not taken him in when he was a small child? The fifth beer stands unfinished at two o'clock. Earl finally nods to a deep but tangled sleep on the sofa with the dull sounds of late night programming coming from the ignored television.

CHAPTER THIRTEEN

EARL WAKES BEFORE JAMES, turns off the television, tidies the living room, and clears away the empty beer bottles. He brews a fresh pot of coffee and slowly sips his first cup standing at the kitchen window as the sun rises in the West and the porridge thickens on the stove. James emerges from his room at six thirty but does not look very well rested.

"I smell breakfast uncle." He takes a seat at the table still clad in his rumpled pyjamas. "Do you eat breakfast every morning?"

"Yup."

"Good." he mumbles. "I like that." He doesn't let on how rare this happened at home in his mother's care, even rarer if she got up before lunch time.

They eat in silence finishing off the porridge, then filling the top of their hunger with toast and Amber's home made strawberry jam. Earl drinks hot black coffee and James has hot chocolate.

"Thought you had to work today? Ain't I going to Amber's house?"

"Taking the day off," Earl answers as he helps James clear the dishes. "Figure it's a good day for a ride out to the cabin. You ever been fishing? You ever ride a quad?" He asks James as he fills the sink with hot water and dishes, both watch as the dish soap creates bubbles around the breakfast bowls.

"I don't think I've ever done anything. Are there any people there?"

"Nope, just us. You go wash up and brush your teeth and get dressed and I'll just clear up these breakfast dishes. Dress warm, a sweater if you've got, or long sleeves to protect against the bugs."

He waits for James to leave the room then calls Amber to tell her not to expect them today. Not wanting a repeat upset from the day before he speaks very quietly so that James will not hear or misinterpret anything that is said between them. He doesn't tell her about the call from Ben last night but does say that he will call again in the evening. After hanging up the phone Earl packs a few lunch provisions in a knap sack. He wants the phone to ring, wants Ben to call, wants to know ....

No call comes. Earl has never been comfortable waiting, to him it leaves him with a dreadful feeling of neglect and abandonment. He will not be found idly lost in empty thoughts while waiting for the telephone to ring. James emerges from his room and the bag is ready so there is nothing to do but go.

With the knap sack and a small cooler to hold the fish they might catch secured on the quad's carrying rack Earl fits a small helmet, bought for David years earlier, to James' head. He tightens the strap until he is satisfied with the fit then he puts on his own helmet.

"This thing only has one seat uncle, and I don't see a seatbelt anywhere. Maybe we should stay home. It looks kinda tipsy. Don't you think it looks tipsy uncle?"

"It is perfectly safe James. I've been riding this quad a lot of years and you'll be safe with me." He steps on, swings a leg over, takes a seat, and slides back. "Just as safe as riding in the truck." he reassures.

"Then why we need helmets?"

"Makes up for no seatbelts. Come on over here and I'll show you."

Earl reaches out to pick James up under his arms and sets the boy on the seat in front of him with his short legs straddling the fuel tank ahead of the seat. He wraps his left arm around the child's small waist. With his right hand he turns a key and the four wheeled machine purrs to life. It is well tuned with thoughtful hands and does not roar or rumble or shake. It has a low calm hum as it idles, and does not hardly even jerk as Earl squeezes the throttle to power it forward.

Before long the two guys are moving through the forest on the quad on a well worn trail. James eventually relaxes, at ease with his uncle Earl's skill of the machine and expert knowledge of the woods. Earl drives the four wheeled machine slower than he would on a solo trip and is careful not to make James at all fearful.

The deeper they travel into the darkening forest, leaving worries on the trail behind them, the more comfortable and relaxed they both are feeling. Tall trees at either side of the trail sway in the wind and guide them forward. Bugs and birds living among wild flowers encourage smiles of anticipation of woodland delights yet to come.

Shadows come to life between the poplars and the pines, songs are sung by unseen swallows, and squirrels chatter a warning of the intruders in the woods. As the terrain becomes more rough and natural, less wheel worn, Earl slows the machine and stops at the edge of a clearing.

Acres of wild flowers and tangled weeds blanket the rolling slope of this hidden meadow. A green overgrown pond sparkles in the sun's bright morning rays and a haze of tiny flying bugs hovers over the shallow water on the far side of blue green water.

Earl is about to say something to James when a brown whitetail doe and speckled fawn emerge from the woods at the far side of the clearing. He catches his words and he and James watch the wild animals in reverent silence. The deer approach the pond disturbing only the mosquitoes, they drink at the waters edge and move across the meadow. As they disappear into the trees only yards from Earl and James' vantage the low purr of the quad engine seems no threat to them.

Earl then drives the quad forward across the same clearing and down a hidden path that the deer had emerged from. They continue their trek almost twenty minutes more without talking until the trees thin, the road begins to slope, and then the old cabin becomes visible. Within strides of the cabin sand and gravel at the edge of the Peace River warms beneath the bright morning sunshine.

"Look around if ya like but don't go in the water. The current is very fast this time of year and the water is cold."

Earl set the child down next to the machine after turning off the engine. James pulls at the helmet, struggles, then waits as Earl unbuckles the chin strap. They set their head gear on the smooth red seat of the quad.

"You heard what I said? You gotta stay on the river bank. That water is icy cold."

"I hear ya uncle." James says absently, his attention on his environment, taking in the beauty of the rushing water and surrounding nature. "I never seen nothing like this ever uncle. Not ever once."

Awestruck, he steps towards the river, then the cabin, then the woods. A brown tree frog leaps from the concealment of the grass onto the gravely path, then hops again disappearing in the leafy weeds and wild flowers. A patch of shrubbery with prickly stems and pink blossoms rustles in the breeze, then the rainbow colours of a leaping fish flashes above the rushing waters of the river. Brown squirrels scurry from tree branch to tree branch. The aging hinges on the cabin door creak to life as Earl enters the little hunting shack with the knap sack he is carrying.

"Hey uncle, wait for me." James runs to the cabin door and does not hesitate before entering. "Wow. Its like a whole house in one little room."

James is compelled to touch everything; old wooden dresser converted for kitchen cupboards, yellow milk crates topped with dusty pillows beside a low wobbly table, bunk beds built right into the walls from mismatched lumber, a steal wheel rim stand supports an oil drum turned sideways. The Drum has a door in the end and a chimney stretching to the low cabin roof creating a hand made wood burning heater. "I would live my whole life in here Uncle. We could stay right here and never go home. Where's the bathroom?"

"Bathroom is outside. Up the hill a bit, away from the water. Don't pee in the water cause that's where the fish live. It's like their home. It's O.K. here I would say, not so great in the winter. Me and Gerald come here lots in the fall. Hunting season. Just you wait, late September when the leaves are changing colours......... Now that's something to see."

As Earl talks, telling James about the last time he came out to the cabin with his friend Gerald, he reaches down two fishing rods from the low dusty rafters above the table and a tackle box from under the lower bunk. James gets down on his hands and knees to see what else might be hidden under the bed. It is shadowy and sleepy in dusty webs and cottony grey balls of nothing. He sees sleeping bags protected in clear plastic trash bags, a wooden crate filled with dishes, a big toothy metal animal trap spotted with the orange and brown rust spots of age.

"Careful under there." Earl warns remembering about the old bear trap. He opens the tackle box and ties floaters and hooks to the lines.

"Come on, let's go fishing. You ever been fishing?"

James shakes his head "no", another thing he's never done.

CHAPTER FOURTEEN

EARL WAKES UP IN a blinding shock of white. Comes up swinging. He has never seen the harsh glaring brightness of a hospital room before in his life. There is the prick of a needle, then he feels ashen, defeated. Against his strong will he falls back, hears the muffled thud of his own head connecting with the pillow. He cannot search out his mother in the room. She appears in black and white and shades of gray, then gone again. He fears he hears Harold's voice, red and angry in the doorway, police officer in the hallway. Closes his eyes and sees a vision of his friend Prince alone in the basement. Fearfully he fights back tears.

How did he get here he wonders, and where exactly is here? Wanting to scream. Straining to remember. It was Tuesday, horrible Tuesday bath night. Feeling the ice of the bath water as he steps in the tub, then dizzy, then black. He shivers in the cool white sheets between the raised rails of the hospital bed. Now his chest hurts, burns, aches, like somebody might have pounded his ribs into jelly. He struggles to keep his eyes open against the weight of woven blankets and the strange comforting warmth of the sedatives, and even in this blinding room full of whiteness he surrenders to dark and comforting sleep.

Almost two years have passed in the blink of an eye since the wedding day. The first day that Harold began turning their home into their prison. Through the enlightening vapour of the next several days Earl surreptitiously learns a few details. His heart had stopped twice but they restarted him, "hypotherm....". Well some new big word that means his heart got too cold and was in shock. His mom is being treated for abuse and exhaustion and got a restraining order for her husband Harold.

Earl don't understand that word, "restrain", but does understand that Harold is gone from their lives and is not coming back. Earl knows it's really true because the policeman comes every day to visit Earl and his mom and ask a few questions about different things. He asks Earl about bruises and bath time and the bed in the basement.. He asks about the telephone and meal times and the abandoned bedroom of a forgotten child.

There are whispers and discussions in the room every day. After a time, not sure how much time, Earl learns he will be leaving the hospital. Knows he should be happy but he is worried because he doesn't get the feeling that these whispering people all in white will let him go back home to his dog Prince. He is not even sure where prince is and he asks every day. Many of his questions hang in the air unanswered. He is very confused about where he will go from here because he understands that his mom is not leaving with him, she will be staying in the hospital longer than him.

New fears replace the old ones and he know more changes are coming. The question of where Earl will go when he leaves the hospital weighs heavy in the air for everyone. Then a familiar voice rises above the other hushed whispers at the door. It is Grace. Earl remembers Grace, Frank's sister. She was pretty and nice and the sound of her voice in the hospital hallway outside his room fills his heart with relief and his eyes with tears of happiness like he has not felt in a very long time.

"Look, he doesn't have to go to any foster care. Do you know what foster care would do to him? I'm going to take him home to take care of him. I insist, I'm taking him home." Arms cross defiantly, insistently.

"He's going to need a lot of specialized care. It's a lot to take on, you're practically a child yourself. His mother will be in this hospital at least another two or three weeks, at least, then she'll have her own treatments and therapies. The courts may not allow her to have him back right away. Were talking months."

"Then I'll appeal to the courts but I'm not leaving without Earl."

Earl can see them at the door of his hospital room. Grace looks older than he remembers. The other lady who Grace is arguing with has a pinched pink face and wears a dark grey pant suit.

"He hasn't seen the inside of a school in two years miss, he's practically illiterate. There will be behavioural problems, socialization issues, maybe depression and anger management care. I don't think you realize what were dealing with. He's been living in a basement like a dog."

"Look lady, I'm old enough, I have a child of my own on the way." She rubs the small bump of her belly. "I know that every child, and especially this child, needs to be with people who love him. Doesn't he need to feel safe and loved? Isn't that what's most important right now? The rest will come." She makes no effort to hide her emotion or her building tears. "Without someone who loves him you're the one who is jeopardizing his future. He needs family and I'm telling you I can be that, I am willing to do all that. I am here and I am willing. Whatever he needs." Grace passionately pleads her case.

"Of course that is central to his recovery but let's face facts. This little boy needs round the clock care. He has mountains of medical needs; head lice, throat infection, ear infection. I've never seen a case this bad. These are not your average childhood illnesses. He may even need surgery, his ears may have permanent harm from the lack of medical attention for these infections. There may be permanent damage to his hearing." The woman moves away from the doorway of Earl's room. He can no longer see them but he strains to hear every word that they are saying about him.

"There will be emotional recovery, counselling and therapy. Not to mention his education, it will be like starting an eleven year old in kindergarten. He's going to act out. Do you think you can really handle that? Cases like Earl's can be very tenuous even explosive, sometimes violent. I don't think you've thought this through. The foster care system is designed for cases like this...... ."

"Look lady, he's not a case! His name is Earl. I love this kid like my own brother and if he's going to be put through all that ....., all that scary stuff, then I won't allow you to make him go through it alone. I know you're doubting my ability, I know I'm young, but please. I know I can do this for Earl. Until his Mom is ready. I'm here and I'm staying. As long as it takes."

"Miss, that might take months. She is not at all healthy; not physically, especially not emotionally. It's more than this child's temporary care on the table, this may be a custodial issue." The woman whispers.

Earl does not understand a lot of what is being said; custodial, recovery, infection. They must be important words because they are very big. He is pretending to sleep, eyes closed tight but under the blanket he crosses his finger and, for the first time in two years, Earl hopes.

"I can do this, I'll meet with every teacher and every doctor and every therapist he needs. I'll get him to every appointment. My husband Ben is away working but I guarantee he is one hundred percent behind me on this. I have all day every day to give to Earl. I can take him where ever he needs to go. I want this. I already took the dog in. I'll sign any papers, whatever it takes. I'll talk to Ella. I'll talk to his brother Art, I'm sure he wants the best care for Earl." she pleads tenaciously.

The social worker is silent. Grace can't quite tell if she is winning the woman over or not.

"My brother was his best friend." Grace adds. "He needs that right, he needs his friends again, and his dog, and love, and time, and people who care. I care and I can give him all of that. He knows me, he will trust me. I'm the only one coming here and standing up for him. I'm here! I showed up and I'm here and I'm not going anywhere. Doesn't that count for anything?."

"I can't promise you anything," the counsellor gives in a little, "but maybe we can try it. I'll have to discuss it with his mother. She's planning to contact her older son Art. Look I'll let you know."

"You know where to find me. I'll be right here at Earl's bedside."

Grace stays at Earl's side after that, leaving only to tend to her dog Buster and Earl's dog Prince. His mom, realizing she has no other options, none available to consider, would side with Grace on the matter. That made the decisions to follow much easier.

At first Art feels that foster care could possibly be the best option, after all Earl has practically been living like an animal. He thinks his brother might even be a danger to Grace and the unborn baby she carries. Grace is persistent and charming and stubborn eventually swaying Art her way. After several phone calls with Grace and his mother, Art drives back to the little town he had longed to escape years earlier, and helps Grace make space in her home for Earl.

What Art sees, what his mother and brother have become, leaves him shaken. He had tried to stay in touch but Harold had blocked every attempt. He spoke on the phone to his mother only once since the wedding, she said she was happy. That was so long ago and so removed from the current state of things.

He loves them both. Wishes he had tried harder to stay in touch. Wishes he lived closer. Wishes he could handle his brother and take him in and care for him. He knows it would not be practical to take Earl to his home; another province and another city where everything would be strange and frightening.

On a warm Summer Sunday Art arrives at the hospital in the morning and chauffeurs Grace and Earl to Grace's house. Art is only able to take a few days off from his work, and will not be staying around. He does however go to his mother's house to gather some of Earl's things, toys and clothing. There isn't much remaining there to get. He doesn't recognize any of his own more happy childhood in the shambled remains. He is heart broken to see that it is not at all the same as the loving home that his mother had worked so hard to provide for he and Earl. He is deeply saddened as he walks through the house he remembers growing up in. It looks to him a stark shell of what he remembers and leaves him in despair to imagine the life his mother and brother shared here with Harold.

It seems like Grace is the only option when it comes right down to it, besides there is absolutely no arguing with her. Her mind is set. Earl is very happy that Grace has won him because he doesn't want to live with strangers. This too gives Art and Ella much relief. Grace's house is near the school where Earl had attended first grade. Some things in the neighbourhood are familiar, a corner store and playground. Grace's home is small and cozy with a picket fence and trees in front, and a vegetable garden and a dog run in back.

When they arrive there from the hospital Prince is there, bathed and fed, waiting at the gate alongside Grace's tan Bulldog Buster. Tails and tongues wagging they greet Grace and Earl. Earl fights back tears. Tries not to, but he cries openly to see his dog once again.

CHAPTER FIFTEEN

"JAMES, I GOTTA TELL you about something. It's about your mom. Your dad called last night when you were sleeping."

They have been fishing from shore for almost an hour and have two shiny trout in the fish cooler. Earl thinks they will make a good supper, James agrees. He has never caught and cleaned and then cooked anything and the prospect of such seems very promising. They fish in virtual silence spare a basic instructional introduction to the sport from Earl, and shrills of glee from James when the fish take the bait and they are reeled in. There seems to be no need for conversation. Earl nets one catch and then the other, bringing the resistant fish to shore without much fuss or comment.

James remains silent as Earl speaks about his mother's condition. The contentment of fishing has gone. He thinks he should be sad that his mom is in the hospital but he really is feeling nothing. Just the warm sun on his face. It occurs to him to try to look sad but nothing happens and so he just stares at the fish in the insulated plastic cooler on the sandy ground between them. At length a question arises in his thoughts and he asks it without apprehension.

"Is she going away like grandma Grace?"

"Your Grandma had an aneurism, nobody saw that coming. Your mother's been very sick for a long while. That's not really news to you I guess. If you're asking me if she's going to leave us like Grace did then I won't lie, that is one possibility. There might be other possibilities. We won't make any guesses O.K., let's just wait until your dad calls again. He will tell us what is happening."

"Uncle," the child whisper, "I like it here with you a lot. I feel happy when I think about it. Is it wrong to be happy now? Every day I'm happy and sad."

"It's fine James. That's fine."

"Happy and sad". The boy murmurs through a single breath. "Every day I'm both."

After the talk Earl packs up the days catch and carries the fishing rods to the old cabin. He tries to get James to open up even though the boy clearly doesn't want to talk either. The limited conversation falls flat over lunch. A lunch of cold brown beans and wieners.

Following lunch Earl makes a few repairs around the cabin, preparations for the coming hunting season. James wanders somewhat aimlessly, stomping through the underbrush and whacking at trees with a big hard stick. It crosses Earl's mind to stop James' seemingly destructive outburst against his surroundings but then he figures it's better to let the boy get his frustrations out. It's what he thinks he would do in this situation. James continues to punish the trees of the forest until his stick breaks against the black trunk of a poplar.

The ride back home is tranquil as the sun sinks down towards the forest and wispy clouds form in the sky above. The afternoon shadows grow long.

By the time they get back to the house James is asleep in Earl's arms, exhausted by the novelty and strangeness of his new and changing living arrangements and by the sad news of his mother. Earl knows the boy has nodded off by the weight of the small body slumped against his chest and the tell tale slowing of the child's heart beat. He has to adjust his hold, wrapping his left arm around the sleeping child and steering the quad with only his right. The ride home takes a little more time, time for Earl to think about his own changing life. About this new responsibility and all the unexpected emotions that have sprung up like a Spring garden, weeds and all.

Back at Earl's home Earl lays the sleeping boy on the sofa after gently removing his helmet. Outside again, he stores the Quad in the garage, then takes the days catch inside to the kitchen to prepare for a late supper.

He chooses to season the fish lightly with salt and pepper and broil them in the oven while he prepares pan fried potatoes on the stove top. He considers not preparing a vegetable, wouldn't bother if he were just cooking for himself. Decides to boil some frozen peas he has stored in the freezer from Amber's garden harvest the past fall. James is just then waking from his afternoon slumber as Earl sets dishes out on the table. As James washes up and Earl fills their plates the telephone rings.

Earl answers. It is Ben calling.

CHAPTER SIXTEEN

"Her parents are flying up to help me with the funeral arrangements. They should be here sometime tomorrow. They are both so old. They shouldn't have to deal with this kind of thing, it was so hard calling them and telling them. I promised them that I would take care of their daughter and I failed them. I called them this morning after she went. She went early this morning. Doctor's say undetermined causes so far. She was so beat up, a lot of drugs in her too. I found some stuff hidden in the house. You name it, stuff I never imagined and right here in the house where James might have gotten into it. She was so damn sick with this addiction. She just wasn't healthy. There is nothing good left, she used to be good and that's all gone. The police are investigating. Don't expect much though, if you know about that sort of thing. It's far worse than I thought, I guess I had blinders on to how she really was. Was just trying to keep my head above water and......, and take care of James. I was still trying to deal with losing my mom. I guess I was just trying to ...., I don't know, ... Whatever I was trying to do, it didn't work. Whatever I thought I was doing it didn't change anything. So now she's really gone." His ramble loses steam and finally begins to falter.

"And how are you doing Ben?"

"No time to tell. This whole week has been a surreal volley of breathless moments strung together with babble and confusion. I don't know which way is up anymore. She went from being a wife and mother to exposing our son to her drug addiction and those people that she was getting this stuff from to being a missing person. I got James out, you know, away from this mess. I don't know how it all started or how she ever knew any of those people or that kind of life. How did I not see these things clearer? I feel so stupid, I didn't see any of this coming. She's gone and all I have left is our son. Thank God he's safe there with you and not here. Thank God for that."

Ben pauses in his long-winded tangent, suddenly at a loss for words. There is an emptiness in letting go, a worry that when something is lost it may never be found again. He once loved this woman and had envisioned spending everyday of his life with her. There's no turning back and nothing left to regain. He struggles for a voice to express himself for the gratitude he feels at not having to have his son there witnessing the devastation he is feeling.

"Thanks to you Earl, thanks to you James has a safe place to stay while this whole ball of yarn unravels and me with it. That's how I feel, that's how I'm doing. I've gone from hiring a divorce lawyer to a P.I. to a funeral director. All that in a short matter of days. It feels like a lifetime Earl. The only thing I can count on now is that she is truly gone."

"What's next?"

"I think I'm still planning on selling the house. I don't want to stay here now. It doesn't feel right to be here anymore, we were going to be a family here. We were going to build a life here. That's all destroyed now. I feel like I hate this house. I think….., I'm too weary to make any decisions. I haven't slept since I got back, need to sleep and talk it all over with James. I don't know what else. I better talk things over with James. Is he there? Has he been asking many question?"

"It's all pretty new and confusing for him, not just his life there but here too. It's a whole different way of life than what he had in the city. He is as much caught in this whirlwind as you are. Just reassure him that things will settle down. Try to sound like you know what is next on the horizon or something. You know, a hint of stability, brighter days ahead. That's what I think."

"Thanks Earl, you're right of course. Put him on then so I can talk with him."

James, having finished eating his dinner while Earl had talked with Ben, swallows the last of his glass of milk before leaving the table to take the telephone receiver from his uncle Earl. Earl sits at the table but fails to taste the food as he gous through the motions, chews and swallows. He listens to James' side of the ensuing conversation with Ben, watches sad eyes well with tears, stifles his own emotion. Watches clouds of angry confusion furrow the child's brow and remembers a time past when he was a child, angry, and confused, and lost. Remembers with great fondness the person who helped him make sense of his own childhood fears, Ben's mother, Grace.

At length James and Ben exchange sentiments of "I love you" and James hang up the black telephone receiver.

"You want to talk?" Earl asks straight out.

"I don't!"

"Maybe later?"

"Don't see why. Not really."

"Why's that?"

"Nothing we can do about any of it. Talking won't change a thing. Not any one part of it."

"Maybe later then?" Earl repeats. He goes to the fridge for a beer and a Root Beer soda. "Let's just sit out on the stoop then James. We don't have to talk at all right now."

CHAPTER SEVENTEEN

THE FIRST DAYS ARE the worst for Earl. The first days at Grace's house are nothing like the calm of the hospital where the kind nurses catered to Earl and he was too frightened and out of his element to act out or rebel very much. At the hospital there were sponge baths and hot meals and no dirty basement. It was nice, but very strange, not at all like he was accustomed to.

Earl just wants to go back to living his life the way he had been; the way that had become darkly comfortable. He wouldn't actually say that he missed having to sleep and eat in the basement with Prince but it was what had become comfortable and normal for him. He does not want to be in the brightly lit kitchen with Grace and eat from the pretty dishes as he sits uncomfortably in the chair. He can't go back to what he knew and now every day, three times a day, they battle over how to eat meals. There is yelling and screaming, bribes and coercion, pleading and punishment.

Most times it ends one of two ways. When Grace wins she eats with a knife and a fork and a plate at the table and Earl sits in the corner with his dog and goes hungry. When Earl wins he takes his food in a bowl to the dark corner of the porch to share with the dog and Grace eats at the table with a knife and fork and plate. Occasionally the chaos of the challenge wins and only the dogs eat, lapping the spilled offerings from off of the kitchen floor.

Meal time confrontations are contemptuously divided by an endless strings of doctors visits, psychiatric evaluations, and meetings with teachers and tutors. The results from the daily onslaught of scrutiny only leads to more appointments, additional meetings, and further prying evaluations. The environment sometimes changes but the mood stays the same, tense and confrontational.

Earls ears both require immediate surgery, the result of months of untreated infections having scarred his ear drums leaving him close to deaf. He is treated for a multitude of ailments that any average child should never have; head lice, flea bites, and unidentifiable scabs and rashes. His head is shaved to allow his scabby scalp to heal and despite his terrifying fear of water Grace must bath him daily. She usually chooses to sponge bath Earl at the kitchen sink, it is by far the least hassle. Bath time is never a hassle free event. After having to be so docile and obedient to Harold's demands Earl now is free to express his pent up emotion. He is free to yell and cry and hit and sometimes run away. Every action becomes enveloped in defiance. Grace's resolve and patience are tested at every turn.

Earl's intellect is tested, his I.Q. test results are alarmingly low. He is categorized as borderline retarded. None of the teachers and tutors they meet with are willing to take on the challenge of a near deaf eleven year old with angry behavioural problems who can't even recite the alphabet and eats with his fingers from the dog dish. In fact Grace is often asked why this child has not been institutionalized.

Every normal thing that Earl had ever learned before Harold had entered his life now seems lost. The letters of his name, the laces of his shoes, the bristles of his toothbrush; all foreign and difficult and buried under a mountain of anger, fear, and dysfunction. Everyday simple tasks like brushing his teeth or tying his shoes are frustrating events that take forever for Earl to accomplish if at all even with Grace tolerantly assisting him.

On top of everything that concerns Earl, Grace is trying to help Art with the sale of Ella's country home and the purchase of a little cottage in town. The telephone rings daily from the realtor and the moving company wanting to make their arrangements. Art lives in the city and his help is mostly in the form of discussions with Ella and the bank. Earl, having become accustomed to an extremely quiet home life and the strict order of Harold's rules, is hugely bothered by so much activity and noisy disruption. This seemingly unending clatter, the constant ringing of the telephone or the doorbell, leaves Earl agitated and highly confrontational. Without the language skills to express himself he develops a "fight or flight" stance, either breaking things or hiding. He is very good at hiding.

Grace falls to her bed exhausted at the end of every day. Days most often ending in battles over the washing of hands and brushing of teeth at the bathroom sink, never ever at the bath tub, and then Earl curls up on the floor in the porch to sleep with his dog. If Grace and Earl are awake they are at odds with each other. There are no times in the day without some conflict or battle of wills between Earl and Grace.

New behaviours develop, bed wetting and destructive outbursts. Broken dishes and slamming doors become daily rituals of conflict resolution where no conflict ever gets resolved. Earl is becoming increasingly aware that his will goes against all expectations but he resist any change from what had become routine and comfortable.

Harold's way had become comfortable and now everything comfortable was no more, taken away. Grace's ways; eating, bathing, and learning are vaguely familiar but mostly foreign to him. The quiet invisible life in the basement was predictable, even manageable, and now it is all gone. Like his mother is now absent so is everything else that Earl thinks he needs.

Grace realizes her approach is failing miserably at every turn. She can almost hear "I told you so" around every sharp corner. Grace isn't considering giving up, not really, but she doesn't see any light at the end of the tunnel. Then, nearly two weeks in, it comes. The answers she needs arrives when her mother appears at the door with her younger brother, Earl's boyhood friend, Frank.

"Hi Earl, 'member me?"

Earl steps back and reaches a hand out to his faithful and trusted dog. The dog remembers Frank and bounds forward to lick at Franks hands and face.

"Hey Prince," Frank greets, "How's the best dog in the world? How you been Prince?" He drops to his knees and hugs the dog. Prince licks at Frank's face, remembering him and welcoming him like an old friend.

"Hey Earl, when my mom said you would be here at my sister's house I just knew you would have Prince here. Grace.... Can me and Earl go out in the back yard with Prince and Buster? We'll stay in the yard, won't we Earl?"

"Oh. Uh yeah." Caught off guard his defences drop and he diminutively looks to Grace for a sign of approval.

"Go on you two. Me and my mom are going to have tea and chat in the kitchen."

"Got any toys in your room? Some cars for in the dirt?"

"I got a few in the porch by my bed that we can take out." Earl mumbles suddenly embarrassed by the space he occupies in the porch.

Grace waits, busying herself with the tea pot until the boys are out of the house with the toys and the dogs before turning to her mother.

"Mom, I'm so glad you came. I think I've done a terrible thing. I don't know what I'm doing. I don't know how to help Earl. We have all these meeting but nobody wants to take us on. There's no help for us and we desperately need someone to help." She sighs exasperated, "Earl is miserable and I'm at a complete loss." Close to tears, she turns on the burner and sets the kettle on the element to heat.

"Well, welcome to motherhood. You didn't actually think this would be easy did you?"

"I guess not. No. Of course I didn't. I just didn't imagine it would be this hard. You always made everything look so easy."

"Don't blame me." Marie chides. "Seems to me you volunteered for this."

"I just don't know what I can do to get through to him. I've tried everything, everything seems to fail. I don't have any formal education for this kind of thing and I'm running out of ideas."

"Maybe you're trying too hard. Sometimes you just have to let go and let God."

"Let God do what......? Really mom, how does that help?" She sighs with frustration.

The kettle whistles calling Grace back over to the stove. She instinctively glances out the window to the backyard.

The bright mid-day sun is harsh and blinding and it takes a moment of focus to see. Like a modern day version of a dusty Norman Rockwell painting, two boys and two dogs play in the dirt at the gnarled roots of an old Maple tree. Tails wagging, the two dogs pant and paw at the ground where boyhood friends carve trails with small trucks and talk comfortably as though they hadn't missed a day. In the space of the cool shadow that bridges the tree and the fence this childhood reunion seems, to Grace, more like a resurrection. Earl is playing and smiling, not angry, not tense, not hiding.

"Let go and let God." Grace whispers toward the window. "Look mom, look at our boys." She breaths. "Look there in the shade of that tree." She feels such relief she could almost weep for joy. All the battles she and Earl have had evaporate and Grace knows at that moment not to give up hope. She had been pushing so hard for answers. She didn't need to push, she only needed to let go a little.

Grace's mom and brother stay for lunch and Earl sits next to Frank at the table. He uses his hands for his grilled cheese sandwich and tries the fork for his potato salad, just like Frank. Prince sits under the table at Earl's feet even though Buddy knows to stay in the porch when the people are eating.

Over lunch it is decided that Frank can have a sleep over at Grace's house with Earl. Grace's mom leaves for a while, then returns with Frank's pyjamas and a sleeping bag. She also brings something else for the boys, Frank's plastic kiddie wading pool.

"Yeah" Frank squeals, "did you bring bubble stuff too mom. Oh please, please, please, tell me you brought bubbles."

"You mean these?" his mom asks producing two blue plastic containers with white screw tops and plastic wands with rings on the ends for blowing bubbles through.

"Yeah!! Yeah, come on Earl, lets put some shorts on and play in the back yard."

Earl hesitates. He is self conscious of the scars on his legs from Harold's discipline, but Frank's enthusiasm is infectious.

Soon two boys and two dogs are running through the sprinklers and through the shallow water in the wading pool. They blow bubbles and slide on the wet grass, and splash with their feet in the water. They scoop at the water with their small hands throwing what they can at the yelping, barking dogs.

Grace sees her mom off at the front door, then returns to the back yard. There she finds joy, and innocence, and liberation. It is all there for her, floating in the warm afternoon air on iridescent bubbles and cheerfully bursting on blades of grass, and wet noses and wagging tails. She runs bare foot on the green grass with the children joining their imaginary play where a bath is not a bath at all. Where triumph is disguised in the cloak of a friendship that had not faded in time lost, and where hope is reborn in children's laughter.

CHAPTER EIGHTTEEN

As THE EVENING DISHES are washed and set in the white plastic rack to dry Earl and James talk a little about the coming days. About what happens at funerals, and what they can do to be of help to Ben.

"Do you know your days of the week James?'

"Some, a little, but they get mixed up."

"Well, come here and look on this calendar." Earl's kitchen calendar shows a picture of a man in a red plaid shirt in a canoe reeling in a big shiny fish from the rushing water of a river. There are lines of squares with numbers in them and at the bottom of the page it says JULY.

"Each line of squares here has seven days in it, and each day has a name. Today is Monday. Starting tomorrow I'm gonna work for four days; that's Tuesday, Wednesday, Thursday, and Friday." Earl rests his index finger on each square as he counts off the days.

"On those four days I will take you to Amber's house in the morning after we eat our breakfast together. Then I will come back to Amber's house and get you when I finish work. It will be supper time when I come back. You will have lunch with Amber at her house."

"That will happen for four days?"

"Yes, you got it, four days." Earl holds up his hand, fingers up and thumb tucked in behind. James mimics the gesture with his own small fingers.

"Four days. I can count to four."

"After Friday it will be Saturday. I don't work Saturday and you will not go to Amber's on Saturday. Saturday you and I will travel into the city to your place, your dad's house. It'll be a long day of driving like when you came here with your dad. Sunday follows Saturday."

"Church day is Sunday ain't it?"

"Church day, yes that it is. Sunday we can rest and help your dad and your grandparents, that's your mom's mom and dad. They will also have traveled a long way too. It will be nice for them to see you and we can all enjoy Sunday together. Then the day after Sunday is Monday. Your mom's funeral will be Monday. That's seven days. That's one week."

"What if I mix it up? I think I already forget."

"Not to worry, I'll tell you each morning what day it is and I'll show you on the calendar. I'm gonna be here for you every day. Then next Monday I stay with you for the funeral and for the whole rest of the day. Your dad is gonna be busy and he will need us close by so we will just stay together and help him when we can."

"I remembered before. When I got here I remembered you from my grandma's funeral. We didn't talk or anything, you talked to my dad, but I remembered your face. I remembered your face in the back of the crowd. You were sitting in the back. When my dad brought me here I remembered that I seen you before that way."

"That's pretty good. You're right there, I was sitting in the back. You have a real good memory. If you can remember that then you won't have much trouble remembering this." Earl places his hand on the calendar. "Nothing to worry about, just seven days. We'll do it all together." Earl reassures as he tries to ease James' worries.

Leaving the calendar in the kitchen Earl pours a glass of apple juice and grabs a bottle of beer from the fridge then follows James to the front porch to watch the sun going down. They just get settled when a green Ford truck turns into the driveway waking dust clouds under the tires.

Dry driveway dirt rises then settles as the truck rolls towards them. Earl recognize the truck, the quad in the box, the greyhound dog, Boomer, riding on the passenger side of the seat with his head out the window. As the truck approaches the house and stops Earl stands and give Gerald a quick wave.

Leaving James on the porch for a moment Earl goes into the house and returns shortly with a beer for his friend. He hands the beer bottle to Gerald and reclaims his seat next to James.

"Gerald.", Earl acknowledges.

"Earl.", Gerald responds opening the beer.

"You were at the church." James says to Gerald. "You're my uncle Earl's friend, aren't you?"

"That's right." Gerald answers. Turning to Earl as he sits and sips at the beer, "The boy has a good memory."

"Yup, he does, we were just saying as much."

"I'm gonna remember seven days. My uncle Earl is gonna help me."

"Seven days?"

"I was going to call you. James and I are gonna have to drive into the city this weekend. His mom's funeral will be in seven days." Earl reaches out and touches the child on the shoulder reassuringly. "We're counting them days together on the calendar. She went yesterday."

"Sorry to hear it. My condolences on your loss James."

"What's caldolantseses uncle?"

"Condolences?" Earl remarks. "Condolences just means Gerald is sorry that you don't have a mom now." Earl swallows some beer. "Gerald, can I count on you to keep an eye on the place when we're gone?"

"Earl, you know better than to think you have to ask." Gerald sips at his beer again, then makes a sweeping hand motion towards James, beer bottle still in hand.

Muted tears are sliding down ashen cheeks. He raises his juice glass to his lips but does not drink. He lowers his glass again but does not set it down, does not brush away the obvious tears. The reality is much sharper when he hears it out loud. He does not have a mom no more.

"Damn sorry boy." Earl speaks softly. "Damn sorry."

He takes the glass from the child's hands and sets it down with his half drank bottle of beer on the green plastic milk crate next to him. With utmost tenderness he moves James to his lap, wrapping his arms protectively around the little child. There they remain, Earl rocking the chair gently back and forth beneath the glow cast down from the porch light, watching as the sun sinks down and the sky darkens. In time the boy falls asleep. As James sleeps in Earl's arms the men pass the time drinking their beers and talking about hunting trips past and times like those that are yet to come.

CHAPTER NINETEEN

AMBER'S FARM IS NOTHING at all like uncle Earl's country home on the acreage and much more like what James had expected a real farm to be like. Much, much more.

The first time he had been there he got to meet the stock dog and her puppies but, as James learns on Tuesday morning, that was a very tiny part of the whole operation. There is so much more to see and do. As Earl drives away after dropping him off at Amber's front door James is immersed in the sights, sounds, and smells of the busy rural production on a real farm. He could barely contain his excitement and curiosity.

"Oh it is good that you got here now, ..." Amber exclaims "you're finally here. I already milked the dairy cows, but I figured I'd wait till you got here before I done the hogs and chickens. I'll tell you though, they don't much care for waitin'." Her brisk but friendly approach adds to James' excited curiosity.

"You got chickers?" James asks.

"Chickens." She corrects.

"How many kitchens you got?"

"Three hundred, give or take. I have three hundred chickens."

"Wow. That's lots. Why so many?"

"That's how many I need to make a decent profit. More so, that's how many I can handle working on my own without having to hire extra hands. I sell eggs and some butcher hens in the fall. The ones that are past their laying prime. I sell milk from the dairy cows, and I sell calves and piglets in the spring. I don't butcher the cows or the pigs because it's lots of work and too much cost. Not enough profit for the costs involved."

As they talk they walk. Briskly and purposefully, across the yard. James sees brown and black cows out in the pasture, and pink pigs in a different pen. Amber walks a hurried pace, he is almost running to keep up with her. James doesn't understand everything Amber is telling him, she talks as fast as she walks and uses a lot of words he never heard before. He has never been on any farm before, there are so many questions he wants to ask.

"How come the pigs and cows ain't livin' together like in my picture books Amber? Don't they all live together?"

"They ain't friendly like that. They all like to keep with their own. It's not like you see in the books. Now it's real noisy in the chicken barn so stay close so you can hear me alright."

They walk across the dirt yard to a really big barn, it's red just like in the picture books. James is astounded, he has never seen anything like it in real life, only in his books. When Amber opens the big red double doors and they are assaulted by a wall of clucking noise and fecal stench. Amber continues talking but James is awestruck by the sights and sounds inside the barn and barely hears a word she says. So immense is the scene before him that he can barely move his feet to keep up with her.

Row upon row of wire boxes fills the expanse of the barn, many many cages, each containing a single chicken. Boxes and boxes of chickens with pathways in between to walk down and to roll the carts through. There are fifty chickens in each row, twenty five on top of twenty five more. There are six rows back to back like that separated by three wide isles. Below the cages eggs tumble down into a metal trough. Amber produces a wheeled cart, and she and James move down the isles and collect the eggs. Some of the eggs get cracked or break on the way down. Cracked or broken eggs go into a bucket under the cart. When the cart is full they put it in a cold storage room and get another one to continue the task of egg gathering. Occasionally they stop to inspect a chicken, if it looks or seems unwell Amber takes the chicken to a separate pen at the back of the barn where it can wander freely and stretch it's little chicken legs.

When all the eggs are gathered Amber pulls some leavers to the side of the barn and water and feed is automatically dispensed into troughs for the hens. Another lever is pulled and water floods out beneath the grated floor washing away all the chicken poop underneath.

"Some jobs are easy, feeding and cleaning in here is one." Amber explains. "Damn hard when the power goes but I got a generator now for back-up. All that we just washed out will be stored and processed and then hauled out in a tank with a sprayer to fertilize the fields. It saves me time and money cause I don't have to get to town and buy store bought fertilizer that's just mostly made of chemical stuff. This farm is natural, all organic. Now we feed the culls."

"Culls?" James asks. He doesn't know the word "organic" either, but culls is easier to repeat.

"Culls are the sickly and lame ones we just moved to the back, it's like a little chicken vacation. I feed them by hand so I can see how they are doing. When they are feeling better they go back to the cages. There are always a few empty cages. Next we sort and stack the eggs."

Back in the cold room Amber and James gently handle the eggs as they sort them into egg cartons. Earl's assistance slows the process but Amber is impressed with how careful the little boy is being and she tells him so hoping he hears her praise over the sound of hundreds of happy clucking chickens that are enjoying their feed.

"When the sorted eggs are stored and ready for a freight truck to take them away Amber and James take the cracked eggs in a wheel barrow over to the pig pens and add them to what Amber calls "chop and slop". The big sows and little piglets happily devour their chopped feed. The chop is mixed with the broken eggs, shell and all, and other feed from one of the granaries. James laughs to hear their grunts and to touch their noses when they poke them against the wooden fence boards.

Next they ride on Amber's green tractor to where hay bales are stored in a pole shed. It's scary for James because the tractor is so big and loud, and there aren't seatbelts or helmets. They stab a big round hay bale on the forks of the tractor, lift it up in the air and drive to the edge of the cattle pasture where the cow are waiting. Amber drops the bale over the fence.

James waits on the big green rumbling tractor while Amber climbs down to the ground and over the fence to take the twine off of the bale. She has to push the large beasts out of her way with her hands as they too gently push to get near the bale. James thinks this is scary because the cows are so big. He thinks Amber must be very brave to push the big cows the way she does.

When the tractor is parked they go back to the house. It is already lunch time and James can't believe how hungry he is. They wash up then say a prayer of grace at the kitchen table. They eat bologna sandwiches with mayonnaise on home made bread and canned peaches with cottage cheese for dessert. James never had such a good lunch with homemade bread and sweet peaches from a glass jar. He eats everything and has a second helping of those wonderful peaches.

After lunch Amber tells James she will have some paper work to do in her office and needs to make some phone calls and so he can watch cartoons on the television for a while in the living room. James likes that idea, so far he is enjoying everything about being here at Amber's farm. Everything is new and exciting, chickens and pigs and cows that he only ever saw in picture books until today are all right here where he can see and touch them. And homemade bread like gramma Grace used to make. He thought there would be more exciting stuff after lunch but is happy that Amber has the cartoons on television. Besides, he has not brought any toys to play with.

James climbs onto the couch and Amber finds a television station with children's programming and a show that James likes called Sponge Bob Square Pants. James swiftly drops to an exhausted sleepy nap there on the couch. Amber leaves him alone in the living room and goes up to her office on the second floor of her house.

CHAPTER TWENTY

EARL'S LIFE CHANGES FOR the better in the comforts of Grace's home. Life gets better for everyone every day. Her brother, Earl's friend Frank, is allowed to come over to Grace's house to play lots, and after a time when Earl is feeling more confident he even goes for sleepovers at Frank's house, always with Prince of course as inseparable as ever. Frank shows Earl how to hold a knife and fork proper, a forgotten skill, and Earl shows Frank how to tie his shoes.

When Earl learns that Frank can't yet do this task he practices all day one Sunday with Grace's help trying to remember, he knew that he knew how to a long time before. On Monday when Frank comes over Earl teaches Frank how the bunny goes around the tree. That feels really rewarding to finally know something. Grace hugs him real tight and tells him he is a good student and a good teacher.

After the first sleepover Earl starts sleeping in the bedroom on the bed. He discovers that it is actually a lot more comfortable, and Prince sometimes sleeps on the floor in the bedroom and sometimes in the porch with his new friend Buster. Prince starts eating with Buster, and Earl starts eating meals at the table with Grace. He likes the conversations they have in the kitchen and he isn't embarrassed to be there no more because he knows how to use the utensils now and how to sit in the chairs, and there isn't anyone like Harold telling him he can't be there or that he does not deserve these luxuries.

Grace teaches Earl how to help with other things that regular people usually do; clearing the table, grooming the dogs, and making his own bed. They do a lot of things together and helping is fun for Earl. Earl doesn't have to do any things by himself, they are almost always together. He is happy to help now, not like before when it was mostly out of fear and worry. He is excited to be learning things because he never has to do things alone and there is no yelling or slapping if things don't go right, they just try again. Both he and Grace are definitely having much happier times now.

Grace's husband Ben comes home from his work on the oil rigs sometimes. He is never there for long, always away to his work, but when he is home he plans fun things with Earl. He takes Earl and Frank and Prince and Buster to the park, and twice that summer they go camping.

The first time Earl doesn't care for camping much. It reminds him of living in the dirty basement and having to keep the fire going and not having any choice in matters. He doesn't think he wants to try again but he does and the second camping trip is more fun. There is sleeping outside under the stars and sandwiches made out of Graham wafers and chocolate and marshmallows, and howling loud at the moon with the dogs. Ben catches four fish that trip and Earl tiptoes up on and catches a wild pheasant which he compassionately lets go. Quiet as a mouse, Earl had learned in his other life how to sneak and not be seen or heard. Frank catches nothing because Frank is not very good at being quiet. Ben says either he will learn or he won't.

There are still lots of meetings with teachers and doctors and talking about how things make him feel. Eventually Earl decides that he likes having feelings, in his old life in the time of Harold he didn't have the luxury, but he would rather not have to talk about his feelings so damn much. Every day they have to talk about feelings and everyday is too much. In time even that becomes easier.

By the time school starts in September Earl can remember his whole alphabet and count to one hundred without Frank's help. The ear surgery, a partial success, makes it so that Earl can hear his teachers pretty good, and he is able to do most of the thing that Frank can do because he has relearned and remembered almost all of the things he didn't need to know in the time of Harold. Earl can't remember feeling so good all the time but then school comes and school presents some new challenges.

School is problematic, but also enjoyable. Recess and lunch time are the best parts. Earl seeks out Frank at every chance to ask questions about things he still doesn't understand. The crowd of kids at school is sometimes intimidating for Earl. They stare at him and he thinks the other kids see his scars and scabs even though everything is healed up and his hair has grown back still he bears a self conscious awareness and worries that others see his past.

There are a lot more people to deal with too. All summer he only had to deal with the people he knows like Grace and the ear doctor, here there are a lot of strange faces. It is definitely not like staying in the basement with just the dog. This new life is nothing like the times of just him and Prince alone in the basement. Mostly Earl seeks out Frank because Frank is his best buddy, the most friendly face in the crowd, and Frank understands him.

Even though Frank is two years younger the two boys have some classroom time together and both boys like that. Mostly though, except for recess and lunch time, Earl spends his days "one on one" with a special teacher who is there just for him. She's nice but the work seems very hard. There are things he knows; colors, shapes, numbers. Mostly there are things he has some ideas about but can't quite recall; adding, subtracting, and basics like catching a ball, running a straight line, or talking about his thoughts and ideas.

That communicating of his thoughts and feelings is most difficult, for two years under Harold's rules Earl only ever talked to his mom and his dog. He likes that it's just him and the nice teacher mostly, but sometimes in the school yard other bigger kids call him Retard, and Dummy. Sometimes smaller kids too. He does know what that means and it makes him sad, and scared, and angry.

Three other new things happen in Earl's life in late September. First his mom finally gets to leave the hospital. Earl's brother Art had picked out a little two bedroom place on a quiet street not far from the hospital for her to live in. He had some minor repairs done, hired a boy to keep the lawn mowed, and had her modest assortment of furniture and belongings moved in. Grace and Maria and Earl and Frank spend two whole days cleaning and arranging furniture and things at Ella's new house in town so it will be nice when she gets there and she doesn't have to worry about that stuff. The doctors have said that it is very important for her to have no worries and stress. They say she needs a lot of calm and quiet. Earl doesn't understand this because all there was when they lived with Harold was quiet alone time.

She has to see her new doctors lots and she can't work because of "mental distress", but at least she gets to be at home. For Earl it means that sometimes, when Ella is feeling up to it, he can have dinner or sleepovers at his mom's new home. It isn't fun or anything, she is sad on the couch in the dark mostly, and she forgets how to play. He didn't want to at first even though it was his own mother the idea of going there seemed scary, but just going sometimes was quiet and good. Earl doesn't mind sometimes and he still gets to live at Grace and Ben's house the rest of the time. He likes that part best.

Grace gives birth to a baby on September twenty-fourth. A boy! He is pink and bald and toothless, and he sleeps a lot. His name is Benjamin Stewart Wallace Junior, or little Ben for short. Earl is glad for the "for short" because Benjamin Stewart Wallace Junior is a mouthful. Now that there are two Ben's. Earl calls them big Ben and little Ben. Little Ben is amazing; small, soft, brilliant.

The third thing in late September, the best thing from Earl's point of view, is when big Ben takes Earl out hunting for the first time. They didn't even take Frank. Just him and Ben driving the dirt roads in Ben's pick-up truck after the first early snowfall of the year. Earl is excited about the day ahead as they unload Ben's quad from the truck box, just he and big Ben. They navigate through the golden Autumn forest painted with an early dusting of snow on some of the open fields, eventually traveling down the banks of the Peace River to an old cabin at the river's edge.

"I ought to buy a piece of land out here Earl." Ben proclaims. "There's no place on earth I'd rather be. I'd fix up this cabin and come out more often for sure. Look around if you want. Just stay back from the water, it's cold and the current is very fast."

"You don't have to say that twice to me Ben, I surely don't care for cold water. I'm not going near there." Earl pulls at the helmet, struggles, then waits as Ben unbuckles the chin strap. "Why do we need helmets for Ben?"

"Makes up for no seat belts I guess." They set their head gear on the leather seat of the quad.

"I never seen nothing like this ever Ben. Not ever once."

"You wanna look inside?" Ben asks as he is pulling the rusted metal handle the of the dilapidated cabin causing the hinges on the door to moan and creak in protest. Dust swirls in the disturbance.

"Cough. Gross, it's real dirty in here." Looking around Earl does not see much that interests him. There is an old wooden dresser, yellow milk crates, and an oil drum turned sideways on a steal wheel rim stand with a round door in the end. He can see that it is meant to be a wood stove with a chimney stretching up from there to the low cabin roof.

"It's a fixer upper, that's for sure. Where's the bathroom?"

"Outside. You can pee in the bushes. Hunting season would be great if this was more liveable. I'd just stay out here all weekend."

"Reminds me of the basement sort of, but I see it's got potential the same as camping. Little bit of fixin' up, maybe some real windows to keep the birds out."

"I brought you cause I see how patient and quiet you are. I think you'd make a real good hunting buddy." Ben compliments Earl. "I seen how good you did sneaking up on that pheasant on our camping trip and I could use a good hunting buddy. That would be way better than hunting all alone. You ever been hunting?"

Earl shakes his head "no" he hesitates, then adds, "I ain't ever done nothing but I'd be your hunting buddy any day." Enthused with the prospect. "Will I lean to shoot a gun?"

"Of course you will. I will teach you with mine and when you are good enough we can go shopping together and get you one for your own."

CHAPTER TWENTY ONE

JAMES IS ALONE WHEN he wakes on the couch in Amber's living room, and this causes him to think of his mother, and those thoughts make him feel cross. He wanders the emptiness of Amber's unfamiliar house looking for her, but feeling strange in this big house he does not call out. Just looking he does not find her and his irritation grows. He is feeling captive in this house just as he feels captive in his sadness. Why does he have to be here with people he doesn't know and places he doesn't understand. So much is strange and foreign and there is no place to hide, he longs in that moment for the safety of his dark bedroom closet and the security and comfort of a closed door.

In the kitchen James opens the fridge door; no juice boxes and no pizza pops or pop tarts. A big jug of orange juice sits, ominous, on the wire rack. Too heavy, he manages to set it on the linoleum floor without spilling very much. He looks for a glass but can not find one within his reach. To the bathroom, he turns the tap and drinks from the bath tub faucet until the water turns from cool to hot. Floors creak, shadows skulk from behind more shadows, walls close in, uncomfortable and itchy in their stifling existence. It is all so foreign and increasingly he wants only to be away from this strange place.

His thoughts wander as he quietly explores the unlit spaces of Amber's big farm house in silence. He longs for the security of grandma Grace's little cottage on the quiet street in the city suburbs where he used to play in the cozy little rooms while she baked cookies and unabashedly sang out loud; "so the Lord could hear". James could not remember ever feeling alone in his grandma's house. James could not remember feeling as alone as he did in this moment, not ever.

"Why can't I go home and be with my dad? Why am I even here?" He boils inside. He feels hot, anxious, and strange here. Annoyances build into angry frustration. As he wanders out of the house, into the enormous farm yard James' anger at the situation builds to a rage against everything that has turned his life so terribly upside down.

In the back yard the stock dog and her pups bark and whimper for the boy's attention. He goes to the enclosure and unlatches the door but is immediately overpowered and assaulted by the on-slot of tiny hounds that rush and push at him with their paws and noses. In his building frustration James tries to escape them running as fast as he can across the yard to the only other place he is at all familiar with, the chicken barn. Out of breath he pulls hard on the door handle and manages it open enough to squeeze through; the puppies follow on his heels but their mother is left outside as the big door close under it's own weight.

Amber now hears the barking of the mother dog and leaves her second floor office to investigate. Downstairs the bathtub tap is running steamy and hot, cupboard and fridge doors hang wide open, and so does the front door of the house. She sees no sign of James outside in the driveway. Her gaze wanders the empty farm yard then her eyes are drawn to the open door of the dog run and beyond there to the chicken barn where her stock dog barks frantically and scratches at the base of the closed barn doors. Curious, walking then running towards the frantic sounds coming from the barn. Screaming child, excited barking puppies, chickens in an uproar; she opens the door to complete feathery mayhem. Puppies scramble outside to their mother followed close by the now red faced child.

"I hate you, I HATE YOU!" the child blasts as her runs past towards the security of the house. Stops but does not enter, arms crossed standing on the doorstep.

She doesn't respond, too busy rushing puppies away from the barn and back to the dog run with their mother. Then, after a quick survey of the damage done inside the barn to the injured hens, Grace closes the barn door and marches in the direction of the house. James squares his stance, wipes the tears from his reddened cheeks, and prepares for her discharge. His mother would have slapped him crimson.

Grace brushes past James to the kitchen and picks up the phone. She talks to someone named Pete for a moment, hangs up the receiver, then brushes by on her way to the wood shed. James is now feeling more confused by her seeming indifference towards him than any earlier feelings of being scared or angry. Grace carries a large block of wood from the shed and places it in on the dirt driveway in front of James.

"Sit!" she demands.

At a loss for words, and still angry, he sets his behind on the edge of the stump and re-crosses his arms in a firm huff.

Grace bring more things from the shed. Several pieces of dried fire wood, a large axe, a metal wash tub and a red plastic bucket. She takes it all in the wheel barrow over next to the burning barrel. As Amber builds a fire in the barrel and fills a metal tub with water from a garden hose, placing the tub on top of the burning barrel, a truck pulls in the drive.

"Pete, Elsie, glad you could come so quick." She greets the two very old people getting out of the rusted Dodge. "Not too big of a job, but could always use a hand and there's of course no time to waste. You know how I hate for my animals to suffer."

Pete and Elsie look to James to be as old as God, except the pictures of God at the church were bright and shiny and Pete and Elsie are worn out and grey looking. Pete has more whiskers on his face than hair on his head and Elsie's gray hair is pulled up tight on top of her head like she was trying to pull the wrinkles out of her face. If that's the case it sure didn't work. Pete is thin as a rake, his plaid shirt and bib overalls hanging from his boney shoulders. Elsie is as wide as a fridge and looks like she might be hiding one under her big yellowish bed sheet of a dress. They both have thick glasses with plastic frames; Pete's frames are black and Elsie's are lime green.

"Pete you can go ahead and get started." Amber directs with a wave towards the barn as she rolls her shirt sleeves to her elbows.

"Start what?" James wonders aloud.

"There are only about five hens injured. They are in the barn, I haven't had time to round them up though."

"Not a problem." The old man rasps, heading for the barn doors.

"James, you listen up now. Pete is gonna bring the chickens out one at a time and I'm gonna take their heads off. After their head comes off your job is to catch them and take 'em to Elsie. She's gonna gut them and pluck the feathers and clean them by the fire cause she's gotta singe them. All you gotta do is catch them and take them to her."

"OK." James grumbles, a failed attempt at mimicking Pete's raspy voice. He wonders about the "take their heads off" part but doesn't dare ask. Seems like a pretty bizarre thing for her to say though. Maybe, he wonders, she's too mad to say it right.

"You're gonna have to run fast, you understand? Run fast and catch them. Then take them over to Elsie. It might be a little messy. You don't quit when things get messy though. Don't be scared or nothing and don't quit. Just do your share and we'll all do ours."

"Yeah, OK, I got it already. I don't quit." defensive, cross, and confused by what she is telling him. Not fully understanding. As if! As if they run with no heads, he wonders. "I just run and catch them chickens that got no head and take them to her. She is going to clean them and burn them. The entire scenario seems ridiculous to him.

The first chicken arrives in Pete's protective arms. It is bloody and one wing hangs down awkward and unnatural over Pete's arm. In a flash and flurry it's neck is laid out on the wooden chopping block at Amber's feet. Amber swings the axe high above her head and drops it down swift, and just as she said it would, the head comes clean off.

The headless hen lays still on the ground for just a second then stands, staggers, and flees. It half runs and half stagers this way and that, head off and broken wing dragging in the dirt, some blood spurting from the open neck. The world is still, dust blows across the farm yard, dirty tired looking farm folks stand motionless, the chicken stumbles, then falls dead to the brown earth.

"Run over there and get that one James. Run and get that hen." Amber calls to him.

James catches his racing breath but his feet are frozen and he can't believe his eyes. Amber shouts out to him again, Pete is already walking an old man shuffle back to the barn to bring another injured chicken. In the fog and confusion James moves to the dead chicken and grabs it's dusty white feathered body. Too heavy he lets go, grabs its waxy yellow chicken legs, then he drags it to where Elsie sits near the fire with a tub of now hot water beside her on the ground. Not knowing what to do, James drops the dead bird at her feet. Then he returns to the stump to sit and wait with arms crossed for the next hen to run headless through the yard. He is momentarily transfixed by the droplets of red blood on his white running shoes.

Elsie guts the dead bird, saving the heart and liver in the red bucket and tossing the rest of the innards into the burning barrel where they sizzle and fry with a nauseating, stomach turning stench. She then dips the bird in the steaming hot water and begins plucking. White feathers pile at her feet. Pete arrives with the next injured hen. The bird is bleeding from a dog bite to its back. Amber raises her axe above her head and drops it down to the waiting chopping block. The second headless hen runs zigzags. James runs zigzags.

Five times over they repeat the process. Pete and Amber help Elsie with the plucking and singe off the left over bits. James is sent with clean plucked, featherless birds to the house. One by one he lays their still warm bodies into a bathtub full of cold water. Cooling bodies turn white and the water swirls pink. Outside a refrigerated truck arrives to take the morning eggs to the market and daily life on the farm goes on.

After, when everything has been cleaned up and put away in the shed and the only evidence is the acrid stench of smouldering feathers wafting from the burning barrel in the afternoon heat, they all sit in the shade of the porch and drink orange juice with ice cubes from the big juice jug. Pete is the one to explain to James that dogs and chickens don't go together and that injured hens can't get fixed by the animal doctor so it's best not to leave them suffer and to make use of the meat they can offer by butchering and cooking them for supper.

James, now past his dumbfound shock; apologizes to Amber. He feels the responsibility for the chicken deaths. It is a new awareness for death but much different than the loss on his mother and his gramma Grace. Amber accepts James' apology and hugs him in her arms and follows with a kiss on his forehead. She also apologizes for leaving him alone and then they all discuss the purposeful life cycle of animals that live on farms; chickens, cows and pigs alike. James is fascinated by this; humbled and also captivated.

After Pete shows James how the tendons in the chicken leg works the talons of the feet while Amber and Elsie bag the cooled hens for the freezer, all but one. Pete and James gather the afternoon eggs and drive out to the pasture in Pete's old truck to check the cattle while Amber and Elsie prepare the last bird for dinner with fresh picked garden potatoes and carrots. Earl arrives just in time for the evening meal. Amber's eighteen year old son David drives in the yard down the driveway just behind Earl.

James is sitting next to old Pete in Amber's lawn chairs and excitedly shows Earl the grizzled yellow chicken foot that he has saved. He tells Earl everything that has happened, rambling with his new knowledge, eager to share. He shows Earl how the long chicken toes can be operated by moving the back part of the foot before they wash up to eat. Then all six people go inside. They gather around the dinner table in Amber's big country kitchen, and there is still lots of elbow room.

The whole meal is set out in the centre of the table and dinner plates are at every seat, even the glasses and cutlery. None of the food was prepared in a microwave. James is astonished to learn that Amber doesn't even own a microwave, she cooks everything on the stove. Earl says a prayer of grace before they begin and pours his beer into a glass instead of drinking from the can the way he does at home.

James never ate dinner like this, not with lots of people talking and laughing and passing the food around. Amber and David smiling, Pete and Elsie sharing stories about the old times. Earl cutting up James's chicken meat for him. Everyone cheerful happy. James is content and smiling, not angry about his mom, or his changing life, or anything anymore.

CHAPTER TWENTY TWO

DAVID STAYS OVER NIGHT that night at his mother's house as is sometimes his habit on his days off from his work in town and Earl brings James over again the next morning. David and James tread to the attic of Amber's farm house that next morning allowing Amber to tend to the farm chores on her own the way she normally would without any little boy to slow down her routine. In dust covered boxes in the attic David and James rediscover the treasures of David's childhood. To James' delight David digs into the old cartons and produces Lego blocks and Hot Wheels cars, marbles and playing cards, Tonka trucks and comic books.

Despite the twelve year age difference the two become inseparable for the next two days. They spend mornings playing with toy cars and trucks in the backyard, tiny roads are forged through the tall green grass, miniature fortresses emerge from tree stumps, and dry dirt becomes a mud-bog obstacle course. Afternoons, when the hot sun is high and burns down on them, they retreat to the house to build and destroy Lego creations. An afternoon snack breaks the time of Lego with more peaceful endeavours when David explains things to James about life on the farm that James doesn't understand and sometimes reads his old comic books to James. Sometimes they talk and play Go Fish with a tattered old deck of cards.

"David, do you have any Kings?"

"No, go fish."

"David, where is your daddy?" James asks unabashedly. His thoughts are unedited and weightless. "How come he doesn't take care of your mommy and keep you safe?"

"He's gone," David responds lightly. "He's been gone a long time. Do you have any fours?"

"No, go fish. Where did he go? Do you have any nine's?"

"Don't know, he left a long time ago. Here's a nine, go again."

"Do you have any two's? My mom is gone too, but she can't ever come back. There's no fix for her. That's makes me sad but not as sad as my gramma being gone."

"Well then you got your dad and I got my mom. That's really something to be thankful for. No two's, you go Fish."

"Don't forget Earl. Hey look I got a two, I get to go again. I got uncle Earl too. You got any ...... what's this one?"

"That's a Jack. The "J" is for Jack."

"You got any Jacks? We got uncle Earl too."

"Yeah, and he sure is a good uncle to have for any boy. Go fish."

"Why don't Earl have a boy of his own? How come he's just a uncle and he ain't nobody's dad with a mom an stuff?"

"Well being an uncle is pretty important stuff, and having a wife and being a dad takes a different effort. Maybe Earl will be a dad sometime and maybe he won't. Maybe he'll just keep on being a uncle to boys like us cause that's the best thing that he can be. I sure am glad I get to call him uncle, he's the very best uncle I could ever want. I know he ain't a true blood related uncle but that don't matter so much to me, not as much as just getting to call him my uncle."

"You got any Jacks?"

"Go fish."

"I'm tired of cards, can we go outside?"

"Sure, I'd like that too. I bet those puppies could use a bit of exercise. We can take a walk down the driveway to the mail box and they can run around a bit."

"Yeah."

James is not really tired of cards, but he's thinking about his dad real heavy just now and it's making his chest ache and his head sad. He's been trying real hard not to think about his dad these past couple of days while they are apart, and trying extra hard not to think about his mom at all. Right now he is really missing his dad. As for his mom, he doesn't know what to think, it's still as confusing as before when she was not gone.

Confusing except now he knows that he don't have to worry about when she's coming home cause she ain't.

It was just as confusing when they were home together, when she was home and he had to hide in his closet. He thinks it's just a little odd that there are no closets in his room at Earls house and also no need to find a place to hide. There is nothing confusing there.

"Let's go play in the yard David."

CHAPTER TWENTY THREE

AFTER EARL REMEMBERS MOST of the thing he forgot he get's assigned a new teacher. The new guys name is Mark Carlson. Mark Carlson is a whole lot different from the lady teacher that Earl had at first. She was OK, but very stiff and teacherly. Mr. Carlson is very different, he has longer hair that he keeps in a pony tail and he wears a sweater with no button shirt or tie. He says to Earl that he looks past limitations, as he puts it, and he says he sees Earl's potential. With Mr. Carlson teaching him Earl doesn't feel confined, it's more like hanging out. Mr. Carlson is just like a normal man, like Earl imagines a dad or a brother or an uncle would be.

Earl can not wait to go to school in the mornings to spend time with his new teacher. A couple times there is a substitute teacher and that means that Earl has to sit in a desk all day and learn from the school books. Grace tells him that this is how to learn to appreciate people, cause when they're gone things aren't the same. Earl sure does appreciate.

Mr. Carlson says he doesn't like classroom walls either so they spend a lot of time outside. They go shopping in the grocery store to learn about math, they go to the playground for sports. Mr. Carlson takes Earl to his home and in his home work shop they do projects for school. Mr. Carlson involves Earl in short easy projects; small engine repair, automotive repair, carpentry, and power tools. He teaches Earl "you don't have to be in a classroom to learn", and "some people learn better with their hands than with books" He calls it life skills. He says it is a better way for Earl to learn and Earl could not agree more.

When the clean up is done at the end of the day they still sit down and write about the work they have done together but Earl doesn't mind this because the work is enjoyable and he only has to write about the fun stuff they did all day. Earl can't wait to tell Grace about his work each day after school, and he is excited to show his mom the things he is accomplishing when ever he gets the chance to see her. It is just not as often as he would like because he has so much to share and she doesn't call very often.

Parent teacher day comes and goes without Ella's appearance at the school at the appointed time. The appointment is rescheduled, Grace attends, but Ella still does not come to the meeting at Earl's school. Mr Carlson reschedules one more time without success. He is insistent that he discuss Earl's progress with her because he thinks it will be very helpful for both Earl and Ella and so, in Mark Carlson style, he plans with a different approach.

A lunch meeting is arranged at a local restaurant. Nothing fancy, no cloth napkins and stuff. Nothing that would be viewed as intimidating; nothing sophisticated or pretentious. A low key truck stop off the highway offering all day breakfast, Mark Carlson's treat. Mr. Carlson brings Earl from school at lunch time and, with little Ben in tow, Grace brings Ella.

Mr. Carlson and Earl arrive first, Earl wants to sit by the window and watch the arriving traffic for Grace's car so he knows when Grace and his mother arrive. He is disappointed when Mr. Carlson chooses a table at the back where the lighting is dimmer, where he feels Earl's mom will be more comfortable and where others will be less bothered if the baby fusses. Grace and Ella arrive soon after Mr. Carlson and Earl and both express their appreciation for Mr. Carlson's thoughtfulness. Ella is particularly glad for a more private and secluded table although she is not at all expressive of these feelings.

Ella's appearance is clean but dull. She is dressed in old baggy blue jeans too big for her thin frame and a grey sweater, the colour reflecting in her face and her hair. Her hair is greying and dull and pulled back tightly from her face. Her only makeup is a bit of lip gloss that matches the gloss that Grace now reapplies on her own pink lips and slips into her shoulder bag.

"Thank you so much for taking the time to come out today to meet with me and to discuss Earl's progress." Mr. Carlson greets the women, approaching Ella with a warm gentle handshake. "I have so much to tell you about Earl's program and the successes that he is having this year." He politely does not mention the difficulty it has been to get her to come for this meeting.

"OK, that's good." She sits. "I don't know how......, why don't he go to regular classes? Can you tell me that?" Her words are clear but low and she does not make eye contact with him. She fidgets with her paper napkin and scratches at her scalp.

"Well" Mark begins, "I feel like Earl has had some experiences that sets him apart from others his age. I feel that sitting in a classroom with twenty other kids would hinder his progress because he is on a different level than those kids, his life experiences set him apart. You understand that what Earl has experienced in his life sets him apart from other children his age?"

She can't help but nod her agreement to this thought. In the air around them spoons in coffee cups tinkle like wind chimes bridging the rigid break in conversation. Ella can't help but wish she were at home and not here surrounded by strangers. Uncomfortably she pulls at her sweater sleeves and crosses her arms defensively.

"I think the concern here......" Grace injects, "is that if Earl is not learning in a classroom he may not be getting all the requirements. That he won't have the basics. Doesn't he need math and language, ... All that other stuff? You know, the basics?"

"Of course, the basics are essential." Mr. Carlson turns to Ella to involve her again.

"As his teacher there are requirements that I must meet in educating Earl. There are guideline that are standard for all students. What Earl is learning is not that different from the other children at his level, the difference is how he is allowed to learn."

"Oh ....." Ella whispers into her coffee cup. "I don't really get it. What does that mean really?"

"Let's be candid. Earl is not all that comfortable in the kind of structured environment provided by the public school system; the classroom. He is different from other kids and he often is teased for those difference by people who don't understand him. He has a lot of trouble sitting still in a desk in a brightly lit classroom for long periods of time, his reading level is not at par with his peers and he would not keep up with those regular assignments done in the classroom. These are facts about Earl that we have accepted and are dealing with directly. We should forget about subjecting him to timed exercises designed for classrooms. We all want Earl to succeed. I am teaching him the things he will need to succeed in a way that fits his learning skills and his needs. This program works for Earl because it is a program that is designed only for him and his unique learning needs. I am addressing Earl's educational needs with a program that focuses on him as an individual."

He pauses, then repeats himself for emphasis. "What I am giving him is designed only for him. I accept Earl's boundaries. I don't ask him to be confined to a desk or to take part in activities that frighten him."

"How do you do that exactly?" Grace asks.

"For example I would never ask him to go to the swimming class with a group because I know how he feels about the water. I know how much you love your son Ella, how far you will go to protect him." He addresses he directly. "I want you to know I respect him and you and I have taken all that into consideration. I want Earl to succeed and feel good about the new direction he is going in his life. I think we all want that and are willing to put Earl first to ensure his future does not reflect his past."

Ella tries to hide her building tears of appreciation mixed with her heavy shame as Mr. Carlson words probe at deeply set emotions long buried. Softly, he continues.

"Earl's program is very hands on, he seems to learn best by actively doing, but that does not mean that he is missing out. He writes about his work every day and he learns all his requirements. Science in automotives and small engine repair, Social Studies in trips to the museum and in selected films we watch together, Language and spelling in the reports he does for every project, and Math currently on a carpentry project his is doing. He's not just getting the basic requirements to get him by, he's getting life skills to take with him into adulthood. We are using what ever we can at the school and also building life skills away from the traditional school setting."

Mr Carlson pauses waiting for more from Ella. When she only looks back at him blankly he looks at Earl a moment as he measures his words.

"You can be proud of your son Ella, he's doing very well, he has accomplished a lot in a short time, please let yourself relax and be proud.

His education is in good hands. I can say that because it's all in his hands, his choices, his accomplishments. Let's not worry about the crust on the bread and lose focus on the sandwich."

"I don't know what that means." Ella puzzles out loud but still with her head down and her face slightly turned away towards Grace. "Really! What's that supposed to mean?"

"I know what it means mom. I know this answer Grace." Earl answers promptly. "Can I tell her what it means Mr. Carlson?"

"Go ahead Earl."

"I'm the sandwich. Mom, I'm the sandwich and it don't matter what I got on the outside or on the edges, just what we put on the inside. Ain't that right Mr. Carlson? What makes a great sandwich is what ya put on the inside. When I learn things that means I'm putting things on the inside."

Just then the food arrives. Everyone has selected from the all day breakfast menu. Earl and his mom are both served pancakes and side orders of bacon. Earl's favourite. Grace and Mr. Carlson have both chosen to have a ham and cheese omelette with whole grain toast.

Earl is sitting quietly, deep in thought. For the first time he quite genuinely wants to share how he is feeling. Nobody has ever talked about him like that. Nobody else makes him feel good and big and strong and in control and smart about things and amazed by his own accomplishments and proud. Everyone is looking at him and staring and he doesn't feel embarrassed or small or stupid, he feels remarkable.

"If you will excuse me," Mr. Carlson stands "I'm just going excuse myself to use the washroom before I eat. Earl, why don't you take this opportunity to tell your mom and Grace about the carpentry project you are doing? I think it is a good project and a good time for you to share with your family about some of the work you can do and the skills you have mastered."

"Oh, well it's a dog house for Prince." he exclaims between chewing bites of bacon. "I picked a plan out at the lumber yard and I had to read all the instructions, and then I bought the wood but I didn't go over the budget, and right now I'm doing measuring, and I gotta measure twice so when I cut I only gotta cut once, and then I'm gonna use some power tools for the cuts and I even got the safety glasses and nails and paint in my budget money, and then………."

CHAPTER TWENTY FOUR

"We have lots of changes in store for us James. I think there will be some really good changes coming for us." Ben hesitates, his son's approval seems central to everything right now. He is wanting more than ever to be the kind of man his son can rely on through these troubled times. "It'll be a whole new start for us. No more bad stuff, we're focusing on new good stuff. A new beginning."

"Are we gonna keep living with uncle Earl?"

"Just until we find a new place to call our own."

"In the city?"

"No, I think not. Not the city. I like the idea of country living. How bout you?

"Yeah, it's nice, and uncle Earl might be lonely without us. We gotta think about uncle Earl now too."

"Earl has told me that his friend Gerald might know of a nice place for sale not far from the church. He's gonna take me there tomorrow to have a look. Says there's a little house big enough for us two, and a small barn, and a shed."

"Is there a dog house there?"

"Well I don't know James. I guess I'll find out tomorrow when I talk with Gerald."

Earl comes outside carrying two beer in one hand and a cup of hot chocolate in the other. He hands Ben a beer and James the hot chocolate then takes a seat in the old brown rocker on the porch to watch the shadows dance across the fields as the sun sinks down in the distant horizon.

The evening approaches without a moon, the blue black atmosphere brightens to brilliant pinks and oranges that stretch into a watery yellow ribbon along the tree line. Forest green and black marry in the silent pines. Three people are bathed in the yellow glow from the porch light as moths flutter in it's brightness.

Lost in thoughts as dark as the distant woods Earl downs his beer in one tip. A tugging on his sleeve brings him back round to the present. James is standing closely next to him. The little boy's face only inches away.

"Uncle, uncle? I said have you been there?"

"Been where?"

"The little house uncle. The little house by the church. Can you say if there's a dog house?"

"Oh, well….. , I guess I don't know. Gerald will say when he comes tomorrow if there's a dog house, or a basement, or what-have-you. Why are you so on about a dog house? You got no dog."

"You ain't got no dog an you got that old dog house. Explain that."

Earl is up and then at the door. He disappears for a quick moment into the house then reappears with another cold beer in hand having exchanged the empty for a full one from the fridge.

"That there….," he begins, still standing and gesturing towards the little structure in the shade of the poplar grove on the West side of the house "is a very special dog house. Did I ever tell you that I built that dog house myself?"

James peers into the darkness towards the dog house where is rests beneath the stand of trees and surrounded by tall grass at the edge of the nearby woods but the child does not respond. Earl sips his beer, slower this time, as he motions for the boy to walk with him across the yard.

"Looks ordinary, but you won't ever find any other dog house like it." Ben gets up from his chair to follow as they step off the porch and strides across the gravel driveway making pebbly crunching noises with their steps. The three stop at the door of the little structure that Earl had built in grade school.

"Only one dog ever lived here in this dog house. I built this house for him and this is where he lived for his whole life." He doesn't add that the dog, his best friend, had died in his arms at the age of seventeen, or that it happened here at this country home. "He was a very old dog. He was my friend my whole life and I loved him. We had a very good life together."

"Did you paint this dog house? Did your dog chase squirrels uncle Earl? Did you take him to the river?"

"He did a lot of things. He liked hunting down by the river very much. His name was Prince. He liked hunting the deer and the prairie chickens."

"I know how to kill chickets.., kickens…, oh, you know." James starts back towards the house ahead of Ben and Earl. "Daddy did I tell you I know how to….?"

"Yes son, I remember your tale about Amber's chickens."

"I think I know how to paint a dog house too. I ain't never done it but I could know how if somebody showed me. I been doing lots of stuff I never done before. I think I'd be good at all kinds of stuff I never done before. You could show me uncle, or you daddy, or even David. I bet David has the time to show me how to paint a dog house."

James' words soften into muttered whispers meant only for his own ears as he sits to finish his hot chocolate deep in the kind of contemplation only found in the imagination of boyhood. Earls takes his usual place next to him on the porch step, creaking the rocker as he settles down to savour the remains of his beer as he quietly recalls the day he lost his best friend, Prince. Ben is silently lost in his own downhearted thoughts just as the others are as he rejoins them on the step and tips his beer to his lips.

CHAPTER TWENTY FIVE

SCHOOL NEVER REALLY GETS any easier for Earl. His teacher, Mark Carlson, is eventually circumscribed into more structured and traditional classroom practices by the school board. Earl struggles with these confinements put on him as though the walls of the school represent undetectable walls to his ability to learn. His progress slows considerably. Mr. Carlson perseveres in his efforts to teach Earl within those structures and restrictions. He finds the needed freedom he seeks by spending many of his weekends and even parts of summer break with his young student becoming more like a mentor than a teacher even though this personal relationship outside of school hours is frowned upon by the principal and school board. Mr Carlson persists and no one is more happy than Grace to see the impact of having a positive male role model has on Earl's development as he is maturing into manhood.

Earl sadly comes to the realization that he will likely never fully regain all of what was lost in the time of Harold and that he will always feel like he has been robbed of something important. There are many aspects of his self image that he will probably never regain either in full or even partially. The damage has been done.

By eight grade Earl still struggles with reading and his spelling is grossly below his grade level, but he can rebuild an engine in a matter of hours. He is then three years older than most of his classmates. By grade nine he is performing fifth grade math, rather poorly, but works weekends at a tire shop for higher pay than the ninth grade math teacher.

Mr. Carlson is still somehow able to instil a sense of accomplishment in him for the things he can do well. The man's encouraging guidance, friendship, and direction fulfil Earl's sense of accomplishment and purpose more than anything he has ever absorbs from the textbooks at school. In his formative teenage years Earl learns from his teacher much more than would be found in books; how to shave, dress, and act like a mature young man. Mark Carlson brings out the humanity and compassion that has always come naturally to Earl's character. Most certainly he is getting more from Mark Carlson than from his deeply depressed and increasingly reclusive mother.

At home with Grace and Ben and the baby Earl gradually and graciously emerges from his shell. He never regains a child's sense of wonder but develops a more mature man's sense of self. He is respectful of Grace, gentle with little Ben, and in big Ben's eyes Earl is an equal in many respects and a good and trusted friend.

Earl and Ben hunt often, occasionally Mr. Carlson and Frank complete the hunting team. Earl's tracking and rifle skills improve and then surpass those of the older men. He takes pride in a clean kill. More gratifying for him is being able to provide and contribute to his home and family. As a hobby hunting is a most suitable and satisfying pastime for Earl's quiet temperaments. The sport requiring great patience and resilience. These virtues are two of Earl's greatest qualities of character.

Earl develops a giving heart in other ways as well. Always willing to watch little Ben and play with him. As little Ben grows Earl finds enjoyment in helping to teach the baby; how to feed himself with a spoon or fork, how to play in the back yard sprinkler, and how to sleep in his big boy bed. In many ways Earl feels a bonding connection to the young child. Not so long ago he could relate to the challenges of these new experiences personally. Earl still spends time with Frank. Frank will be Earl's best friend for forever, but the deeper understandings he holds for little Ben's emerging development creates a connection as strong as brotherhood.

And so life goes. Earl develops a gratifying contentment in his life. Life is boring and uneventful, and for Earl that is perfect. He has his family, and the friends he calls family. He has a job he likes and, at school, a teacher who is more like a father to him than any man could ever be. There is school, and work, and hunting, and home; and then there is his mother, Ella, who he tries to visit as often as possible.

Still living alone, she lives on assistance cheques from the government, and does not work. He worries for her. She goes to her weekly counselling but spends most of her time at home in the dark with only the light from the television to guide her well traveled path to the refrigerator. The fridge is full of discount beer and frozen dinners she buys at the twenty four hour market. She does her shopping in the night time when there are few people. There is no sense of security for her in the day or around lots of people. In public, and especially around men, she feels exposed and vulnerable. Harold's abuse has left a deeply scarring insecurity. She wears the feelings of being constantly judged and always inadequate as a second skin and a paper thin armour. From the outside she is thin and modestly attractive to look at, inside, beyond the fortress of walls she has defensively erected, she lives in self imposed isolation.

Yes she is lonely, very lonely, but there is no one she will trust to touch her life or her broken spirit. Not even her son is a viable confidant even though he was a witness to many of her long suffered abuses. She is not an obvious drunk, but she is seldom fully sober. She is comfortable in her existence of quiet isolation.

At the end of Earl's ninth year of school, just shy of his eighteenth birthday, a change emerges and Ella's bitter comfort is thrown to the wind. Her son Earl is drawn in to this whirlwind of change. In his heart there is no other option but to once again guardian his mother.

CHAPTER TWENTY SIX

"Hello. Come in Ella. What a surprise to see you!" Grace exclaims as she opens her front door to invite Ella in.

"Please come in, come to the kitchen and I'll put the coffee on. What an unexpected surprise this is. Earl will be so happy to see that you've dropped by to visit, he and Frank are at the park with little Ben but they'll return soon for lunch." Grace fails to hide her surprise that Ella is visiting her home in the middle of the morning. Normally extremely reclusive, Ella rarely leaves her home in the day time.

"Thank you Grace. Thank you so much. Thank you for being home. I don't know what to do and you're so smart and helpful…. . I guess I thought you would know what to do. I really don't know what to do."

"What has happened Ella? What's the problem?" Grace questions as she pulls her long hair out of her face into a low bun at the nape of her neck. There was a time that Grace likened the older woman to her mother, giving her the same respect. She is still not wholly comfortable in the reversal of roles that has developed between them. Ella now appears a meek and diminutive childlike person more needful than ever. Grace had become the stronger and more stable of the two women.

"Maybe I shouldn't have come. I can figure it out on my own somehow maybe, I just don't know what to do. I'm not good at solving problems. I'm not smart about things like you are Grace."

"Well Ella," Grace can see Ella's growing agitation and anxiety, "why don't we just sit down to coffee while you think. We haven't seen each other for so long, let's just visit and chat a bit, OK."

"You wouldn't happen to have a beer in the fridge would you? It was a long walk and I would really like a beer. A beer would really help right now."

"Oh......." Grace ponders hesitantly. "I think Ben has a couple in the little cooler in the garage."

She leaves the kitchen and returns moments later with a can of Budweiser. Carries the can to the sink, wipes the top off under the kitchen tap before she opens it. Then she reaches for a tall glass in the cupboard, opens the beer, and pours the golden ale into the tall tumbler. She set the glass on the table in front of Ella, discards the can in the recycle bin under the counter and then pours herself a fresh hot cup of coffee and adds sugar and cream. She pulls out a chair from the table and quietly sits across from Ella and waits. Sips at her hot coffee and waits for Ella to begin.

Ella takes a sip of beer and momentarily wonders at the amount of fuss that Grace has just given her lowly beer can. She would have drank it from the can. She never uses a glass at home. She thinks the fuss is completely unnecessary but does not bother to mention. She's not one to complain, besides she has bigger problems today.

"They're givin' me ninety days." Ella blurts mid sip with a little golden liquid slipping down her chin before it is gone with the wipe of her sleeve. "I only get ninety days, then I'm off everything."

"Who's giving you ninety days for what Ella?" Grace probes, slightly confused by Ella's chattered outburst.

"The province! The government! The doctor! My life is falling apart Grace. It's all coming to an end, they don't even care that my life is gonna fall apart." Agitation grows in her voice and her words spill in a quick jumble.

Grace had heard on the news about government changes to the social assistance program that has paid Ella's expenses since her release from the hospital. A program designed to support the unemployable. Grace and Ben and Earl had discussed the implications that those changes might have on Ella's life. Still she waits for Ella to explain it in her own words.

"I went to my counselling this morning and the doctor says I won't be eligible for his help no more, and she says the government is gonna cut me off of assistance and I have to think about finding a job. They think I should be able to work and have a job and I won't need help. Oh Grace what am I supposed to do? I ain't had a job since I was a teenager. I can't do nothing like they want. I don't have no job skills or nothing like that. What am I gonna do Grace? How can they just decide this and I don't get no say in the matter at all?" Her hands shake. She sets the empty beer glass down on the table.

"Well," Grace replies slowly, "Let's take a moment and think about this." She leaves the kitchen briefly and returns with another can of Budweiser. Washes the top then hands it to Ella. Ella pours the liquid into her glass herself then follows Grace's example by going into the kitchen to stow the empty can in the recycle bin. Grace pours more coffee into her coffee cup. She stirs in the milk and sugar. She takes a cautious sip, takes her seat at the table, takes her time, then speaks. Softly and gently she guides Ella through the thought process.

"You say you have ninety days right? Nothing has to be decided right this moment. Three whole months. There's lots of time to examine your options Ella."

"I don't have no options. I washed dishes part time in high school, then I got married to the boy's dad and he took care of me, then he left and I had assistance, then Harold came and took care of me, then I was on assistance again. I'm scared Grace. Maybe you don't get it, I'm really scared. I'm old and I got no job skill. My life is over and you want to tell me about my nonexistent options. What kind of fool do you take me for?"

Grace sips her coffee and then stands and leaves the table. She begins to prepare chicken noodle soup and cheese sandwiches in the kitchen for lunch while she continues to calmly and gently talk to Ella about the local job market. She mentions part time opportunities for someone with Ella skills, and about funding options for skills training at the community college. Ella doesn't think she can work around people or go to school with people or have people telling her what to do all day.

Grace is aware of Ella's limitations but tries to offer positive and constructive council. Ella has always been set in her ways and she has always had difficulty with options and choices. She has always eased into the path that she thinks offers the least resistance without fully examining consequences. She has always busied herself by counting her losses and losing track of gains until, in her mind, there are only losses. No options, just dead ends. Grace, aware of Ella's emotional limitations, tries to offer suggestions that might pose the least perceived challenges or threat.

"Dish washing jobs are away from people and usually in the evening, perfect for someone who is more of a night person than a morning person." Grace tenderly eludes. "Maybe the doctor would give a kind of recommendation to a prospective employer." Another option Grace offers is to find a job with animals, with the veterinary clinic or the animal shelter. Ella likes this idea and actually pauses to consider this suggestion, she is good with animals. Had pigs and chickens at her modest country home. She always loved animals. Grace softly points out skills that Ella has, abilities she has always had as she seeks to broaden Ella's narrow view of her available opportunities.

As Ella's tension gradually softens and her glass is emptied for the second time Grace begins to set the table for lunch. She indiscreetly removes the beer glass and pours Ella a hot cup of coffee.

"The kids will be back soon. Would you like to freshen up before lunch?"

"Oh, yes that is probably a good idea. Thank you Grace." Ella expresses sullen gratefulness beneath her breath as she leaves the room. Grace is a good person she thinks. Grace will fix this mess and help her out. Grace always has good ideas for her. Ella returns to the table in a slightly calmer state of mind.

The boys and dogs return from the park just as lunch is ready and seeing her son triggers a return of Ella's anxiety. Her thoughts and emotions show outwardly in very linear and reactionary ways. She sobs to Earl over lunch about her predicament, and although Grace and Ben were against the idea when it was discussed before hand, Earl offers a suggestion of his own.

"I'm gonna be done school in five weeks, then it will be summer break. Mom I could come stay with you and help take care of things. I got a good job and my boss says he'll give me more hours. I could be making good money with a full time job."

"You mean you want to live with me? Oh Earl if that's what you are saying that would be perfect." She beams. "That would solve everything."

"Now Ella," Grace interrupts, "Earl is just a boy, he's only a teenager. You must not expect to rely on him for everything. He's only a teenager you know."

"But he's such a good boy, Grace. He's eighteen years old now. Practically a grown man. Oh please Grace." Ella pleads the way a child pleads for a cookie. "I won't have to worry with Earl there. Ain't that right Earl?"

"Well mom I do have a job and that's good but you will still have to find a job too." He looks to Grace knowing she is a little disappointed. "It's not gonna be all me mom, we can only do it if we're equal. I can help, I really want to help you, but we gotta do it together. You will still have to find a job, even just a part time job to start with."

"Oh, I understand," Ella hopefully remarks, almost bubbles with new hope. "Don't worry Grace, I know school is important, I know he's too young to take on such responsibility all on his own. I won't let anything interfere with that. He is practically a man you know. He is almost too old for school, but you are right." She pauses in her rambling excitement. "It's important, I know that. But don't you see how good it would be for me if my son could live with me and help me? We could get to know each other better like a real family. He could be a good influence for me Grace. You've given him such good care. It could be a new beginning for me. I would have a family again."

"You have to understand my concerns Ella. Earl means the world to Ben and I. He's part of our family too. You both are. His future means the world to us. To both Ben and I."

"Grace, you and Ben are good people. I couldn't have asked for better for Earl. Really, I mean that. Please let us do this, please just let us all try." The older woman is on the verge of sobbing and Grace sees clearly that there will be no turning back.

"The two of us together, me and my boy. Just think about it Grace, it could be a good thing for me and Earl, for all of us. Oh thank you Earl. You are such a good boy. He is such a good smart boy Grace. Everything is gonna be alright now. Earl will fix everything for me."

"I'm not leaving the country Grace," Earl adds, knowing Grace's worries. "I'll just be across town, and I'll come see you all the time. You and Ben and little Ben. We'll still have hunting, and picnics and fun. I really want to help my mom Grace. This is very important to me too and I know I can really do some good for my mom. I just know it's the right thing. Family is important, you taught me that. My mom really needs her family to support her right now and Art is so far away. I'm sure of this. I'm sure that I can do this Grace."

Grace half-heartedly sets aside her personal objections and tries to offer some encouragement. After lunch Grace's mom, Maria, comes to Grace's house to get Frank. Maria stays for a cup of coffee and offers Ella more advice on the changes she is facing, and the heavy mood of the day lightens.

Grace quietly harbours deep concerns for Earl, she has come to love him like her own son and she has done so much, given such personal extended efforts like a mother would do, how can she just let go? She shares her concerns with her husband Ben when he telephones that evening. Ben's cares reflect her own but he reinforces to his wife that Earl is a grown man and it is time to let go. "Let go and let God."

She remembers when Earl was little and so troubled and her mother had given that same advice. Although she cries herself to sleep that night, the next morning she drops Earl and little Ben off at the park before going to Ella's house to help Ella clean Earl's new room.

CHAPTER TWENTY SEVEN

"THE MOVING TRUCKS WILL be here with our things tomorrow." Ben informs Earl over morning coffee. "James is so excited I'm surprised he can even sleep. That little house by the church will be perfect for us. And soon I'll be starting my new job in town. I can't believe the house in the city sold so quickly. Things are really turning around for the better Earl."

"I'm glad Ben. I hoped they would."

"I was wondering something, wanted to ask you something..... ." Ben hesitates. "I was wondering about that old dog house Earl... ."

"No need to wonder, me and Amber are a step ahead of you."

"What do you mean?"

"Amber knows of a pup. Not one of hers, a different breed. I can help the boy fix up the dog house. It's a good thing to do, right?"

"You're giving him the dog house?"

"And a dog. He'll have to earn it." Earl is firm "He'll have to do a little painting. Maybe you can help us with that?"

Ben nods in agreement, not hiding his delighted grin.

The two men sit quietly and contentedly on the step sipping coffee and looking out across the autumn fields that are waving like a sea of amber hands welcoming them to the day. Sunlight filters through distant trees and hints at slights of green wheat woven through the gold. In ten short minutes the morning sky lightens into brightening blue, young Canadian Geese rise in the distance in a familiar V pattern of flight, and distant traffic stirs a grey cloud on a far country road.

"Hey dad," James calls, bursting through the front door. "Ain't ya cooking breakfast yet? Daylights burning and we gotta get to our new house and start livin' there! Today's the day ain't it?"

"Not today son, our stuff will be here tomorrow. There are things the lawyer and banker gotta take care of too. We'll store our stuff in the shed here until then. The possession date, that's the day we move in our stuff, that's in nine days. We'll count it on the calendar like Earl taught you. In the mean time we got some cleaning and painting and fixing to do. We can do some work and repairs while we wait on the paper work. We'll stay a while more here with Earl."

"Sound like too many days to me dad. Nine is a lot. More than seven."

"We'll keep busy. We're gonna go into town to buy paint and shingles and cleaning supplies today and ...... , and you get to find out about the new school you will be going to soon. We're gonna help Earl with some things too while were here, and he's gonna teach us about hunting. Hunting season starts soon and Earl and Gerald are gonna take us hunting too."

"That sound like lots to do." James muses, "Did I mention that daylight's burning?"

"Come on Ben." Earl smirks as he rises to his feet. "You heard the man, "Daylight's Burning". You brew another pot of coffee and I'll cook us all some breakfast."

CHAPTER TWENTY EIGHT

By the time Earl finishes ninth grade Ella has found a part time job at the local animal shelter and is managing to get by on that and some limited partial government assistance to help her through her transition into the workforce. The assistance is temporary but she takes it as long as they'll give it. She could maybe get by without the assistance now that Earl is moving in with her but it would mean that she would not have the money for extra's, like beer. She can not imagine one day for herself without beer to sooth her pain and take the edge off.

The first week of July Earl moves his things to Ella's house. It is awkward to start. Although the changes are welcome Ella has lived alone for a long time and has to adjust to the new arrangement. Earl has not lived with his mom for so long it almost feels like he is moving in with a stranger She is certainly not the same woman she was before the time of Harold.

As Earl starts full time at the mechanic shop they gradually settle in to each others life styles. They each find their comforts in this new arrangement. They are, for the most part, content with the new life and between the two pay checks they have more money between them than either of them have ever known before.

For Earl working full time means less time to spend with Grace and Ben, less time for hanging out with Frank, less time for hunting and fishing. By the end of a busy work day working full time hours Earl is tired. Ella's cooking habits are lazy and lacking and so dinner and supper are not the well rounded meals like Grace would have prepared for Earl in her home, but rather a microwave dinner and cold beer with his mom in front of the television. Life is static, uncomplicated, simple and easy.

By the end of the summer Earl and Ella have settled into a comfortable rut and Earl decides to stay working full time hours and not to return to school. Life seems better now than it ever has been for either of them. There is money enough to pay the bills, there is food and beer in the fridge, and sometimes even enough for restaurant take-out. Restaurant take-out is a real extravagance in their modest routine. Earl saves a few hundred dollars and buys a pick-up truck at auction, a rusty fixer upper that Earl repairs himself on the weekends. Ella adopts a kitten, Tigger, from work. Earl and Ella and Prince and Tigger settle down together. Life is good, it is a humble existence but they are secure in the predictability of it.

Grace and Ben have mixed feelings. They are disappointed in the fall that Earl is not returning to school but secretly feel like it's a blessing that he got as far as he has. Farther than anyone had really expected given the way things were from the start. School had been awkward and difficult for Earl, he is now older than many in the graduating class. He is happy to have completed ninth grade and when he learns that Mark Carlson is being transferred to a different school he thinks that he probably would not have successfully completed another year anyway.

Earl is very proud of his job and his work and that makes them glad. His boss wholeheartedly surges with praise for Earl's job quality and work ethic at the shop. He is quiet and diligent, and has developed a rapport with many customers for his no nonsense value approach. By Summer's end many customers ask for him by name and appreciate his work quality while always keeping their cost concerns in mind.

Earl is drinking every evening with his mother, and although Grace is concerned about this habit Ben argues that this occasional drinking has helped Earl to come out of his shell and to be more interactive with people. Ben and Earl still go hunting and fishing and Grace invites Earl and Ella over for family dinner every Sunday after church.

Ella, like Earl, is not especially social, but having a job seems to have helped. She truly enjoys the animals she works with and is happy for them when they are adopted into good homes. The animals at the pound warm to her care and respond to her. She herself feels a connection to these sometimes abused and abandoned pets. There is an unspoken association that translates through her touch and care for them. For the first time in longer than she ever remembers she feels a sense of purpose not reliant on any other person. She finds these feelings very foreign and uncomfortable but tells no one.

Life becomes a mundane stretch of weekends and seasons passed into years. Nothing ever happens but everything tumbles by. Little Ben learns to walk, learns to tie his shoes, learns the alphabet. When he starts to kindergarten at age five Grace takes on a part time job at his school. Ben continues to work his rig job and is not home much. Art moves father away to another province with his new wife.

After two years Ella takes on more full time hours at the animal shelter and they quietly celebrate, it is her first work with benefits. Earl buys a late model Ford Tempo for his mom and two years later a newer Ford pick-up for himself. The sweet relief of uneventful normalcy covers them all like a worn blanket on a winter's night. Changes come, they are gradual and comforting and ordinary.

Earl sometimes has pause to worry, like when the truck doesn't seem to run well or what his boss thinks when he is late for work because he drank a few too many the night before. Sometimes he worries about Grace and Ben because they don't seem very happy when they are together, he worries also about his dog Prince getting old and losing his hearing. Mostly Earl worries about his mom. She is not vocal about her feelings but he has a sense that she is deeply depressed.

She seems alright most of the time, not especially joyful at all, not ever, often lost in grey despondency. He asks, she says she is fine, but she never really sounds all too convincing.

The days when they have to euthanize sick animals at the shelter are worst. She is darker than grey on those days, locked in a funnel of depression bleaker than charcoal. On those days he sees her tears through the dim lighting of the television and hears the immovable charge of despondent misery above the sipping swallow from the rim of the ever present beer can.

She is not outwardly expressive about anything but it is this deeper quiet that troubles her son. Earl once read in a book at school that there are two kinds of madness, the kind that drags you down and the kind that lifts you up; so of course he feels justified to worry about the way she drags herself down. Earl personally doubts that he could handle the information that she keeps to herself. She holds back but if that floodgate were ever opened he fears her pain would drown them both. He has ideas about the emotional abuses she may have suffered by Harold and imagines that exposing certain details of those truths would crumble both his own spirit as well as hers. Still she was never really one to express her feeling, so he tries not to let it bother him when she doesn't and, from the outside looking in the picture seems normal enough.

Beyond those little concerns life rolls out seamlessly. Earl is happy that there are improvements, however minor or small. Most nights he goes to bed content, beer in his belly and cash in the bank, that is more than he had ever expected from life. Most nights Earl can be glad for his blessings; a job, a home, a family, things to call his own. Most nights Earl pushes the little nagging worries to the back of his mind. Most nights he can reassure himself with positive thoughts that life is good when he rests his head on his pillow. In the welcoming darkness that every evening provides, he can set his mind at rest that the sun will rise with him in the morning.

CHAPTER TWENTY NINE

"HEY JAMES........," JAMES' FATHER Ben calls down to him from the roof of the little house they are fixing up. "I think I'll have a few shingles left over, enough for the roof of that dog house."

"Do you think there will be paint left over too?" the child calls back up to his father.

The little house near the church has been the center of activity as Ben and James prepare to move in. Amber comes with lunch everyday and often stays after to do some cleaning inside, washing wall and sweeping out the cob webs of the previously uninhabited house. Ben has repaired some windows and mown the overgrown yard, he is now repairing the old neglected roofing. In the evenings when cooler autumn winds blow in through the thick darkness of the nearby forest they are joined by Earl, Gerald, and David who arrive with paint brushes and ladders, and beer. The exterior siding of the little house is now almost completely transformed with a fresh welcoming coat of white over the old faded yellow.

"Is tomorrow the day dad?" James calls up.

"Yes James. I think by the end of today all of this outside work will be finished. Tomorrow we will be able to bring our furniture and boxes."

He looks down from the hot roof at his son who is enjoying a break in a lawn chair pulled into the shade of an over grown willow patch near the house. "Maybe you should go in and see if there are any cans of soda left in the fridge and I'll come join you for a spell. I could use a break."

"I thought you'd never ask." James calls up to him as he sprints into the house to get a couple of soda's.

Ben is pulling another lawn chair into the shade when his son returns with a soda for himself and one for his dad.

"I bet you'd like to get started on that dog house soon?"

"Um….., well dad…., you can finish the roof. I ain't in no hurry and I ain't got no dog yet, and …, well…, I'd like to do the dog house with uncle Earl."

"I was thinking that very same thing. I think Earl would like that too." Ben nods.

That day, after the evening meal, the dog house is loaded into Earl's truck and moved to Ben and James' new home. By the end of the day both the house and the little dog house have been completely repainted and re-shingled. Ben and Gerald are even able to move some of the furniture and boxes into the little house, brought over from the storage sheds at Earl's place.

The next day is Saturday and all available hands pitch in to move the many pick-up truck loads of furniture and boxes. Although the work done with joyful hearts James quickly tires of this and being too small to be of any great assistance he is often underfoot and is taken to Pete and Elsie's house where he helps them make sandwiches for lunch and later meatloaf and potatoes and gravy for supper. The food is all put in plastic dishes with lids and they rummage everything else from the fridge; pickles, cheese, boiled eggs and pie. Pete calls it a field lunch and talks about farming in the olden days for the duration of the entire drive over to Ben and James' house.

They all eat supper from white paper plates, sitting in lawn chairs and on boxes in the front yard while the tailgate of the truck is transformed into a buffet table. After the meal they clean up and then the men just sit around in the yard talking about times had, and times to come. James rides his bike, recently unpacked from their belongings, up and down the dirt driveway.

Amber and Elsie leave the yard for a while. The women go away together almost unnoticed in Amber's truck. Later as the hot August sun slips toward the tree line and a soft breeze brushes across the goldening landscape Amber and Elsie return. Truck tires roll to a slow stop on the dusty gravelled driveway.

Elsie does not get out of the truck at first, she just sits there not even opening the door. Amber gets out from the driver's seat and walks to the front of the truck, then she calls James over to her. He drops his bike carelessly on the side of the road and curiously approached.

"James, Elsie and I brought something for you. A surprise."

James steps back a bit. In his experiences surprise were never usually good to get. He crosses his arms, says nothing.

"You gotta promise to take care of it, OK."

"Can't promise nothing 'til I know what I'm in for."

"Well, come round the truck and see then."

Elsie opens the door as James approaches the truck. She tries to turn but the carefully hidden bundle in her arms erupts from the truck at this first opportunity of escape after the confinement of the truck ride in Elsie's big arms. There is a yelp and a bark as the gift hit's the ground running, then a black and white ball of fur is dashing circles around the yard, sniffing at tires and nipping at shoes.

James' feet burst after the pup before the boy even has a solid thought about it. He has been talking about a dog for so long and nobody ever answered. He didn't think he would ever get one by the way they all seemed, like nobody cared about a dog except for him. Of course he had been hopeful, but he never would have guessed a dog would be coming for him today. Even after fixing up the dog house, there was no real hint that a dog would follow, and now here's a dog. A real, running, black and white puppy dog. He stumbles on untied shoelaces, lands on his knees, almost on the little dog.

"Is he really mine? Can I really keep him? Mine for real?" He sings out, scooping up the excited ball of fur in his arms.

"Yes James, why else would we make you work so hard on fixin' up that old dog house?" Earl comes over. James releases the pup long enough to hug his uncle tight, but short, around the neck. Then he scoops the dog up again.

"He ain't one of yours Amber. I know that for sure. Where's he from?"

"He's a purebred Collie, comes from a long line of herders from over on the Watson farm. He'll be real smart and since you don't have nothing for herding I but he'll be a real good hunting dog."

"Hear that dad?" He jumps up and runs to Ben. "Come on dog. Did ya hear that dad? I got a hunting dog. Dad, a Collie hunting dog. Dad, do you see this dog? Isn't he wonderful?"

"You gotta name him son. Are you just gonna call him dog?"

"Awe dad, course I thought out a name. Thought one out yesterday when me and Earl was working on that dog house. Uncle Earl says his dog was named Prince, and when I was playing cards with David he told me that a Jack is kinda like a Prince after the King and the Queen. I figured that if any dog was gonna have the honour of sleeping in Prince's house he'd have to be a Jack. I sure didn't think I'd get one this quick though. I sure didn't guess I'd have a Jack of my own today."

"You sure did put some thought in then didn't you?" Pete remarks.

"Jack?" Ben asks. "His name is Jack?" a little confused by his son's rambling line of logic.

"His name is Jack. You hear dog? Your name is Jack." He scratches the pup behind the ears as it bounces at him and licks at his face and hands.

"That's a real fine name James. Jack and James." Gerald comments.

Boy and dog run non-stop for at least another half an hour before both collapse on the front step and Ben brings James a glass of water and a bowl with water in it for Jack. Pete and Elsie produces an old horse blanket from behind the seat of their truck for inside the dog house. James and Jack both huddle inside the dog house to test out it's new comforts.

"Dad? There's one thing I don't understand." James calls out from inside the crowded space.

"What's that James?" Ben asks his son.

"Well....., why do I gotta give him pure bread? Amber said he's pure bread. Don't you think he'll be wanting some dog food?" Everyone laughs as Ben and Amber explain the meaning of "purebred" to James.

That night James puts on his Batman pyjamas and crawls into his bed with Jack by his side, both are exhausted from their busy day. James is a little bit restless. This is the first night sleeping in this new home. His new room has strange shadows in the corners and the house makes strange and unfamiliar noises inside and out. The evening wind sways and rustles willow braches against glassy windows and fallen leaves scratch at the front screen door. Hugging his puppy under the blankets James puts all his little concerns aside. Tomorrow he would have all day to fuss about this new house, new room, new school, new life; tonight he can only reflect on how happy he is feeling as he rests his cheek against his furry new friend and drifts to a contented sleep.

CHAPTER THIRTY

It is a hot and sweaty Friday afternoon at the end of a hot and sweaty July. All of the bay doors at the garage where Earl works are pulled open in hopes for a breeze, however slight, to blow through. Earl has been working on installing a new muffler on an old car. His hands are strong and his movements are led by knowledge, there is no hesitation in his movements, only his quiet confidence. The car is a classic, remarkably well restored, navy blue 1967 Dodge Charger. Earl is thankful for the small relief that the cool concrete floor is providing as he works beneath the car lift.

The car's owner, a guy named Gerald, will be there at three to pick his car up. Earl glances at the clock as he moves out from under the beautiful automobile, the clock on the wall reads 2:57 pm. As if on cue a car pulls up and Gerald gets out, bearded and sweaty from the heat in old faded blue jeans and a cotton tee shirt.

Earl stands inside the cooler pocket of the garage and waits for Gerald. He would prefer not to step one foot outside beneath the intolerable burning ball of fire in the blue and cloudless sky. Thankfully Gerald is more than quick to come inside to settle the bill. Earl lowers the car lift and then meets Gerald by the garage door with his keys. The two men talk a short while, sharing their love of classic restoration projects like the Charger. The bill is paid and Earl hands the keys to Gerald. Gerald goes back out into the unrelenting heat gets into his car and heads out West towards his acreage outside of town. He leaves the parking lot, taking a left onto the busy main hi-way, away from the centre of town. Earl watches him leave behind an older model blue Ford Tempo.

"Hey Earl," a sweaty coverall clad co-worker calls to him, "did you see your mom? She was just here. That's her there driving out. See, right there in front of Gerald."

"No." Earl replies as he turns and takes a second look in the direction that Gerald has gone. "Really? I wonder why she didn't come in to say "Hi" to me. That's kind of strange, ain't it?"

"I don't know. She ain't my mother. I didn't talk to her or nothing, but I think she might of left something in your truck. She was just over at your truck but I didn't see her talk to no one here."

Earl's mother had been on his mind all morning. She had been especially gloomy the day before. It seemed that one of the puppies that came to her care may have been carrying a highly contagious disease. "Parvo Virus" she had said, or something like that. The dog was to be tested and if the test proved positive then on Friday morning each and every unvaccinated animal at the shelter that might have been exposed would have to be euthanized, no exceptions. This upset Ella so much that she had passed on having either dinner or beers the night before. She retires much earlier than usual to the dark seclusion of her gloomy basement-like bedroom.

In the dry heat of morning while watching the hot summer sun rising in the early hours of the day she said the strangest thing to him. Coffee cup in hand she exclaimed in quiet certainty "If the sun does not shine today I will surly die". Earl was unsure what she meant by this because she was looking directly at the shiny sun. As usual Earl let her melancholy statement pass without comment.

Earl now wonders if the dogs and cats at the animal rescue centre have all been put to death and if his emotionally crippled mother had to witness their every end. He thinks to himself that she is most certainly without the managing skills to process anything so hugely unsettling.

Her general mood was one of melancholy but lately, more than ever in the past, small set backs seemed to cripple her and leave her greatly distressed emotionally. She just seemed much more reserved and shut down than usual. The death of one dog or cat would have drained her. A knot tightens in his stomach thinking about how she might react to the obliteration of several animals, possibly more than twenty, that she cared for and had come to call friends. Her closest friends, the only ones she could relate to and even sometimes confide in. In her mind perhaps her only real friends. He hoped to himself that if that were the case she would likely have just chosen to go home to the ghostly comforts of her dark bedroom. He wonders to himself why she would go West when she left, that turn would take her out to the highway away from home.

Even as he thinks these thoughts he has strong doubts. The truth is he has no idea how fragile she is because she never would have talked about such things, not even to him. Especially not to him. Since her social assistance ended she had not been back to share her emotions with her doctor appointed counsellor either. He wasn't even sure of the last time she had seen her regular physician. Earl worries the rest of his workday and even tries to phone home twice but no-one is there to answer the ringing telephone.

At six o clock when the shop closes for the day Earl walks to his truck and finds what his mother had left for him there when she had stopped three hours earlier. A note in an envelope lays on the seat of the truck, white, and warm from the heat of the brightly shining sun. Heat that has amplified through the windshield of the truck. Standing next to the truck with the door ajar Earl's fingertips burn as he unfold the heated page.

"Dear Earl," She has written in heavy black ink. "It has been another bad day. I can not even remember what a good day is like. My life is an unending stretch of misery. More sorrow than cheer. More grief than pleasure. I do not remember one good day in so very, very long. I am of no use to anyone. My affairs are in order, I have made certain of it, and if no one sees this note you will at least have that. Please keep this letter between the two of us only. I am sorry for all the pain and suffering I have caused you in your life. It is all I have ever had to give. I do not want to feel this way any more. I have nothing left to feel. There is nothing else for me to do."

The note is signed "Ella", not love, not mom or mother. Just "Ella". Earl stands there in the parking lot for most of ten full minutes, sweating in the burning sun with the white paper in his trembling hand, not knowing what to think of the words she has written. He is very confused and not fully grasping what she may have meant.

As he gets into the truck and drives towards home he stuffs the paper into the breast pocket of his faded blue coveralls and wonders absently where she may have went after leaving the parking lot of the shop and if she will be at home in her room when he gets there. He drives slowly through the hot streets, stops for a six pack, and is thankful when the radio news reports an accident involving a car and a log truck blocking traffic in the opposite direction, glad that this will not delay him on his route home.

A single blue and white police car waits in front of the house where Earl lives with his mother. Sunlight burns at his eyes as he rolls his truck into the driveway. Ella's car is not there, this makes Earl feel….., he has to really think about it. How does he feel? What should he feel.

Two police officers waiting on the sidewalk, stand sweaty in the late day heat. Their heavy uniforms are sticky. Perspiration is beading against their faces where their dark hats meet their pink foreheads. They introduce themselves politely then ask Earl if he knows where his mother might be.

"When was the last time you saw or spoke to her?" they gently ask.

""This morning." Earl answers. "We had coffee together, then she went to her work and I went to mine."

"You haven't seen her since this morning?"

"No." Not truly a lie. He had not actually seen her when she dropped off the note in his truck. "I haven't seen her."

"Sir, there's been an accident. Is there any reason she would have been driving out of town on the highway?"

"She might have had a hard day at work, she goes for drives to clear her thoughts sometimes." He fibs, knowing she has never enjoyed driving, particularly on the highway. "She mentioned getting a bucket of chicken after work for dinner, there's a KFC out on the highway. Too damn hot to cook."

He didn't want to lie to the police but it seemed necessary to protect himself from the unfolding truth and from the ambiguously damning words on the crisp white page in his pocket. He can almost feel the heat of it burning through his shirt and scorching through to his own heart.

Earl knows what they are getting at with their gentle questions. That is to say he understands the individual questions, but they are like puzzle pieces that don't fit together. In the late day heat and the blinding sunlight, standing on the burning asphalt driveway, Earl is suddenly clammy and sickened with the chill of understanding. The puzzle pieces fall together and the picture they create is blistering and repulsive.

Every question fitting into the next, every word of her note connecting to the accident on the radio news. The picture producing something far too glaring and too intense for Earl to clearly identify in this given moment. He feels like he is falling in slow motion into a long dark hole. Like the reality of what has taken place is softly and gently luring him in the way a hunter lures his prey.

Today will be a haze of what happened, what didn't happen, what might have happened...... . The if only. Everything is colliding in mid air until the captivity of grief fully takes its hold. The appreciation of what has been left unsaid now speaks volumes. Today will be followed by deep emotional poverty, an emptiness engulfed by dry winds through his soul like a howling hurricane that rises up on a dry, hot, sunny day.

No!

More than anything his sudden suffering leaves him blinded and breathless. His only actual frame of reference of this magnitude of pain is the menacing searing that rips the air from a boys lungs when his body is pushed into an icy cold bath. He can feel the icy white chill beneath the burning sun. It feels just like a plunge into the kind of cold that would stop his heart from beating.

"This" he tells himself , "feels exactly like that".

The officers help Earl to the door and guide him inside his home, out of the burning sun. Then they wait by Earl's front door until Grace arrives.

CHAPTER THIRTY ONE

JAMES WAKES UP EARLY, before the autumn sun comes up on the horizon, and wanders outside in his pyjamas with his new puppy. Both boy and dog urinated in the driveway then James walks back inside to get a drink. He pokes his head into his dad's room. Ben is still sleeping. Then James takes an already open litre jug of apple juice from the fridge, puts his shoes on, and goes back outside to find Jack.

The dog is wandering a zigzag path towards the road. Sniff... wander... sniff... wander... sniff, sniff. James loyally follows Jack's aimless path. At the end of the driveway the two turn West towards the church, towards the warmth of the rising sun. Along the way Jack laps at dirty water in ditches and James drinks his juice and finds late season wild strawberries and eats them with childish haste. They walk for a long time, then they lay in the grass at the side of the road for a while. Rested, they walk some more. The sun is now above the tree tops warming them on their outing.

When they come to a new trail that winds away from the main road Jack follows his nose. James follows Jack. The hot sun is now rising higher in the sky and the shade of the trees along the roadside gives generous relief to the two travelers. As they continue forward small shoes and paws crunch in the fallen leaves. Many new sights and smells and sounds come to pass as the forest calls them onward.

Red winged black birds are perched in the high branches, they sing a forest welcome to the boy and dog. Squirrels hop from tree branch to tree branch making chattering noises. Jack is eager to pursue. The puppy jumps at the base of this tree, then that one, yelping to the flighty rodents to come down.

From the main trail they discover a new path going this way and then another going that way. The tall forest trees get thick and hard to move through at some places but then they open up to a new wider clearing, or a new path emerges beckoning the wandering travelers further on their expedition. Just when James is beginning to feel a lonely chill, just when home fleetingly crosses his thoughts for the first time this morning, Jack sniffs out a rushing creek running through the woods. Water gurgles over rocks with beckoning appeal.

The sun is now higher in the morning sky and beats down on large rocks and soft sand providing warm places to rest and to play. Jack laps at the water and since James has long since finished his apple juice he gets down on hands and knees next to the black and white puppy and laps at the cool water beside his dog.

Now they follow the water. There are fewer trees along the creek, it is sunnier and warmer and more open, and there are new things to see. Frogs leap, bugs flitter and fly, it is as though a whole new adventure has begun. The forest was cool and mysterious and hushed, the stream is lively and fresh and bright. Jack pounces after tiny minnows and shadows of minnows, splashing in the warm shallows. James giggles, rolls his pyjama bottoms to his knees and laughingly follows as his shoes fill with the pleasing cool wetness from the stream. This renews and awakens their energy.

As James and Jack frolic, following the direction of the flowing water, the little stream is joined by a larger stream of water. Wider and deeper, the flowing water now runs faster. James slips on the rocks and falls, soaking his pyjamas through and through. Afraid for the first time, recalling his uncle Earls warning from their earlier trip to the big river, the child makes a retreat to the safety of the rocks and sand of the creek bank.

As Jack turns towards the startled cry of his boy the distraction throws his balance. The voracious current of the water is more powerful than the small puppy can manage and the little dog is suddenly swept down the stream, bouncing off of large rocks as he flails his short legs. Desperately he yelps and paws for footing as his little body bobs up and down in the frightening rush of the stream.

With no time to cry of his own wet state James runs over slippery rocks and through some marshy weeds along the banks trying urgently to keep up. Fear grips his heart as he watches his puppy being carried farther and father away. He wants to run out to his little dog but he is too frightened of the merciless water and it is all he can do to keep up as he rushes on the shore and Jack frantically paddles for safety.

In a short time the dog's determined efforts pay off and the soaked little pup crawls from the water into James' waiting arms. They share a great feeling of relief as they hurry from the water's edge. Both are exhausted and soggy head to toe.

A breeze from the water slips under their skins, a shiver cuts through. Clouds begin to form in the bright blue sky above them. James holds Jack tight to his chest, heart still racing fast, and lifts him to a thicket of tall grass away from the cruel stream.

Holding the puppy firm James cries openly and wipes warm tears off from his flushed cheeks with his damp shirt sleeve. He knows without doubt they are in some trouble. Feels the small dog's uncontrollable shiver against his dripping pyjama clad chest. Looking around he sees only tall looming trees and knows at that moment that he has lost the path that will take them home.

The sun and gathering clouds are high above them now and he is unable to control his emotions as he feels more tears streaming down his wet cheeks. Without any blanket of warmth James lays down with his puppy in a place between the churning water and the looming trees and pulls the tall reedy grass around himself for small comfort. Jack licks at James' teary cheeks and snuggles into his chest. The pair of adventurers, now filled with exhaustion; hungry, cold, and alone, yield to a frightful and restless nap as they hide in the false security of the tall grass that surrounds them.

CHAPTER THIRTY TWO

BEN SLEEPS SOUNDLY THROUGHOUT the first night in his new home. He wakes feeling somewhat well rested on Sunday morning. When he sees that his son's bedroom door is still closed he decides to take advantage of the peace and quiet in the little house while he is able. He brews a pot of coffee and takes his first cup outside dressed in pyjama pants, tee shirt, and house slippers. He has become very comfortable with Earl's morning routine of taking coffee on the front step and smiles about it to himself as he settles into his green canvas lawn chair in front of his home. At around eight thirty Earl's truck rolls in.

"I thought I'd see if you and James would join me at church today." Earl greets. "We can travel together if you want."

"Sounds good to me. You want a coffee?"

"Of course." Earl answers pulling up a lawn chair for himself. "Where is James this morning? I expected to see him and the dog running circles in the driveway."

"Not up yet, must have played themselves out last night. I'll check on them before I get you a coffee." Ben says as he gets up and moves towards the door. "I thought that puppy would be scratching to get out and do his business by now."

Ben goes inside, Earl waits on the step for the coffee but instead hears Ben's pace quicken as he moves around the little house. Ben comes outside but does not stop at Earl. He very quickly strides to his vehicle and then to the shed and to the garage. Earl looks at Ben's face and immediately see the growing panic in Ben's eyes. "You sure he ain't playing under his bed or something?"

Both men go back into the house calling for the boy as they search under beds, behind furniture, and in every shady corner. When it becomes clear that neither the boy or the dog are in the house they go back outside calling out the names of child and dog as they explore the out buildings in hopes that James and Jack are hiding somewhere nearby in the yard. When it is harshly evident that they are nowhere to be found in the house or yard Ben begins to truly go to pieces.

The underbrush in the trees behind the house is thick and branches snag at Ben's clothing as he pushes aimlessly, this way and that through the thickness of unkempt vegetation behind his home. Earl takes a brisk walk to the end of the dusty driveway and even bends to his knees to look inside the drainage culvert that passes under the road. Brushing his knees he looks both directions down the road from the driveway, a car approaches from the East, the church pastor pulls up and slows to a stop. Earl informs him of the missing child. The pastor drives away to the church and Earl rejoins Ben at the front step of the house.

"The pastor says he'll send some of the congregation out here. The more help we can get the better. Maybe you should go get dressed and I'll call for help. We will get a search group going right away." Earl telephones Gerald and Gerald instantly springs into action to get to Ben's house quickly. When Ben emerges from the house dressed in jeans and a sweater he and Earl quickly discuss ideas and make a search plan to find the little boy and his puppy dog.

Earl immediately begins unloading his quad from the back of his truck, he will cover more ground this way than he would on foot. Ben phones Amber who also arrives rather quickly with David. Amber offers to stay at the house in case the child returns and Ben and David unload David's quad from Amber's truck. By the time the three men mobilize a few of the members of the church congregation have arrived to join in the ground search efforts. Gerald also arrives with his quad in his truck box.

With thanks to the church pastor, who had urged his flock to help, seven more men arrive to help. The men will search on foot in the areas surrounding Ben's home. Earl, Gerald and David will travel farther reaches on their quads. Earl is the first to leave the yard after gassing up his quad from a fuel can in his truck box and taking a sweater from inside the cab. He stows the sweater beneath the seat of his vehicle. Turning West from the driveway he scans the ditches and tree-line for any sign of disturbance as he slowing makes his way.

Earl drives along the road the three and a half miles from Ben's house to the church and then two miles past that to the next intersection. Not knowing how early the boy had left means he has no idea how far James could have gone. Back tracking, he investigates the clearing around the little country church on foot so that he does not disturb the prayers inside. He back tracks even more slowly East towards Ben's house.

The bright sun is rising higher in the blue morning sky reminding him that precious time is passing. Although he feels the urgency of the situation his unhurried search becomes more prudent and deliberate. Ahead he watches David, who is farther down the road, turn South into a field and leave his quad to look for tracks in the dirt. Earl spies a trail to the North into the forest and without real cause of reason he turns his quad onto it. He tentatively disappears into the woods telling himself to trust his gut and yet knowing the urgency of time should not be wasted on baseless hunches.

The shade of the forest trees is little relief to Earl. He stops and listens but only the moaning of the tall trees can be heard. He checks the travel box on the back of the quad, there are two granola bars, he closes the box without taking anything out. He listens closer to the noises of the woods, birds and squirrels and breeze blowing in the rustling leaves mostly. The sun rises higher, moving quickly towards mid-day, clouds gather and time is wasting. Like blind sheep he know others wander in the woods closer to Ben and James' home. He himself is thinking he has gone too far out, there's no reasonable cause in thinking they might have come this far.

As Earl turns his quad to head back to the main road something bright in the shrubbery catches his eye. He might not have seen it had the sun not glinted through the branches of the trees at just the right angle to make it noticeable. A one litre apple juice box, vibrant blue against the dying Autumn greens of the forest floor. Earl motors the short distance, picks up and shakes the empty box, then he stores it on the back of the vehicle. He turns back and drives deeper into the shadowy thickness of the pines and poplars tangled with underbrush and wild vegetation.

He feels hopeful with little explanation or cause except an empty juice box as possible evidence of a passer-by here in the woods. Still he moves slowly through the growing shadows of the thick trees. He is vigilantly watching for any other clues the child might have left on the trail. Finding great difficulty in the mix of hope and worry, anticipation and fear, Earl stops to listens.

Not wanting to let his emotions dictate his actions he closes his eyes, opens his mind to only what he can hear, and waits for the faintness of the little boys trail to speak. All that he hears is the rustle of branches and the slight babble from a nearby stream.

When Earl was a child he would sometimes go to the stream near his house with his dog Prince. His heart quickens at the memory. He drives a little faster towards the sound of the flowing water thinking about those times, just a boy and his dog. It feels like more than a just a hunch as he drives toward the murmur of the stream.

At the water's edge he turns off the engine and stretches his tense legs as he walks up stream along the rushing water. In short strides there is a bend in the stream and the sandy shore is interrupted by a mix of large jutting rocks and marshy mud thick with tall cat tails. Looking down at his feet Earl realizes that his are the only footprints to have disturbed the muddy ground. James could not have been here. Clouds cluster and darken in the blue sky as he turns back towards the way he came.

Walking a short few steps past his quad Earl furtively scans the area for signs that the child and his puppy had been there. At first there seems to be nothing, but then a few yards farther where the small stream is joined by another rushing flow signs of intrusion appear. Random paw prints on the rocks still damp from small wet feet. A child's shoe print in the sand, pooled with water in the shallow impression. A movement down stream catches his attention, a lone brown coyote eyes him from the opposite edge of the rushing stream. Then there is another movement and Earl knows that he is not the one being watched by the wild canine. In that moment the presence of the coyote is quickly forgotten.

A shivering child stands in the midst of a patch of tall grass in his wet Bat Man pyjamas. His bare feet red with cold, a sopping shoe in each hand. Hiding behind his muddied ankles a now timid puppy, fur damp throughout, shies away from Earl in a whimper.

"Uncle." James whispers, "Is that really you?"

"Who were you expecting?" Earl gently chides.

"Well, I was talking to Jack here but he nodded off cause he got tired from his swim. Then I was talking to my gramma Grace even though she ain't really here. Then I remembered where she was so I just talked to God. It's church day ain't it?" As he rambles he moves forward, drops his shoes, and takes Earl's hand in his.

"Well yeah, it's church day but God can hear ya on every day."

"Gramma could hear me in every room." Stopping a few feet from the quad James hugs Earl's leg. "I was so scared and cold. I didn't think anyone would come and find me."

"I got a sweater here on the quad. Big but it's dry. And a granola bar."

Earl is not wanting James to see the might of his concern and relief. With great vulnerability and humility he turns away. A cold chill claws his spine like past demons pushing in. In a fleeting flash icy waters flood him wholly; heart, body, and mind. With a mighty shrug to shake the past ghosts off he pulls his mind back to the moment at hand. He feels like a bolt of lightening has hit him; sometimes you have to experience faith first hand.

Earl drops his stubborn reservations as he falls to his knees and holds the child. He wraps his arms gently, warmly, tenderly around the boy. Allowing his great relief to let go. James seems to melt into him as they both allow the feelings of relief to be of comfort . Earl feels James soften and holds him there a while. When Earl eventually releases James he mentions the granola bars again. Snack treats that he always has packed on the quad.

"Maybe Jack's a little bit hungry too." He says to James as they both allow their tears to fall. He gives the boy a second squeeze, then moves to the quad and produces the snack bars.

"I'm sure hungry Uncle, we ain't had nothing all day. Probably missed out on lunch too I think. Did we?"

"It's late. Maybe near lunch time, sure, but not by much. I think maybe your dad or Amber would cook us some bacon and pancakes. You best change out those wet pyjama's and we can head home. Your dad got pretty worried when you weren't there and now half the damn church is out lookin' for you. I don't think anyone thought that you could go this far."

"But you did uncle Earl."

"I guess I had a hunch. I just know how it is to be a boy and a dog. It's like an adventure ain't it?"

They remove James' dripping clothes and James is enveloped by the large sweater that Earl has brought while they talk. Earl stores the wet pyjamas and shoes in the compartment under the quad seat while James shares the snack bar with Jack. Earl removes his jacket and plaid over shirt, and then his tee shirt, puts his plaid shirt and jacket back on and then wraps the shivering little puppy in his cotton t-shirt. It is warm from his own body heat.

On the quad Earl sits as far back as he can and places child and dog in front. James holds tight to Jack. Earl is holding both with one arm wrapped around and using the other to steer. They head out slow, back through the thick woods towards the road. Earl drives at a snail's pace at James' request because neither he or Earl have helmets. Jack has never before had a ride on a quad and is nervous and restless. He squirms anxiously in his little boy's arms.

As they move through the forest the trees seem taller to James and the road seems much longer. He tries not to let it but the fear and worry of being lost re-surfaces and he cries just a little into his uncle's sleeve. Earl pulls the boy closer to his chest and slows to wipe a tear from the boy's pink cheek. He does not stop and makes no remarks about crying to the child. The moment simply passes without fuss and James is comforted and glad that Earl is the one to find him and take him home. He has a feeling that he does not need to explain himself as he snuggles into his uncle's protective arms.

When they reach the gravel road Earl stops and shuts off the engine. The sky has clouded over and now there are more clouds than there is blue sky to be seen. He slides back and gets off of the quad, then walks to the front to talk to the child face to face. Wrapped in Earl's large sweater the boy seems very small. Jack squirms and Earl lifts him down, removing his t-shirt from the dog. The little dog pads through the grass down into the ditch to pee. Earl takes a caring moment to adjust the big shirt on the little boy.

"There are going to be a lot of people at your house. Lots of people came out to help me and your dad look for you."

"Are they mad about it? Are they all gonna look hard at me?"

"I will carry you straight into the house. You can go right in and get dressed in your own clothes. I'll deal with the people, you deal with you."

"OK. Will my daddy be angry?"

"I won't lie, he's pretty upset. This kind of stuff is scary for people. Don't matter if you're little or big, people get scared. He's gonna be happy to see you, happy that you got found and that you and Jack are safe now."

"I was really scared uncle. I tried to not be cause I had to take care of Jack, but it was very scary out there all alone uncle Earl."

"I was scared too, but that's all over now. We're together now, and together is always better than alone. There is one thing we gotta do now. You can help me do it if you want. We can do it together. I have a flare gun here that I always carry with me on the quad and I'm gonna shoot it up in the air." He stops talking long enough to load the flare into the gun. "All the folks out looking for you are gonna see the flare shoot up in the sky and they will know that you've been found. It'll tell them that they can stop lookin."

"Wow uncle, that's a pretty big gun. Is it loud?"

"Yeah. It is."

"I think you can do it for both of us."

"I tell you what, I'll just stand over here and do it." He strides three paces away from the child. "Maybe some day when you get a bit bigger I can teach you about guns like your grampa Ben taught me. Cover your ears now."

Earl steps back and fires the flare gun straight into the sky. They watch as the smoky flame blazes through the air as the acrid smell of gun powder wafts around Earl, then Earl stows the gun and the damp t-shirt and gathers the little puppy back into his arms and hands the dog to James. He slides onto the quad behind James and starts the engine to travel back to the house.

"Uncle I ain't ever had a friend like this here dog."

"Oh, how's that?"

"He never left me the whole time. Ain't that amazing?"

"Sure is James."

"Yup! Sure is amazing. I ain't never had that kind of friend. Was your dog amazing too uncle?"

"Just like that. He was my best friend. We were just like you and Jack and we were friends a long, long time."

"I think me and Jack too. He's gonna be my dog a long time."

"Let's go home now." Earl says to the boy as a spitting rain begins to fall. "Let's go home and get some food."

"I'd like that very much uncle. I'm so hungry I'd even eat vegetables."

CHAPTER THIRTY THREE

ELLA'S MEMORIAL IS SMALL and uneventful. In attendance are Earl and Art, and Art's pregnant wife Dawn. They were on an airplane as soon as they got the news. Marie and Frank are there; Frank home for only a few days before he leaves for college in the city. Of course there is also Grace and Ben, and little Ben. There are five people attending from the animal shelter where Ella was employed. They share a common sentiment and describe Ella as quiet, private, and highly sensitive to the needs of every animal.

Art has been very helpful to Earl in dealing with the serious details about the accident report with the police investigator and with Ella's life insurance provider. Earl has not mentioned the note that she had left for him in his truck to anyone, not even his brother. The death is determined an accident. Earl sees no harm in this omission if he and his brother will benefit from her life insurance. He believes this was, when it comes down to it, her last request. He feels some justification in keeping this secret and honouring what he feels is her final request. The only thing she felt she had to give so why take that away from her.

After the memorial Earl saves the note in the back of a photo album behind his mother's death certificate. He feels good about keeping her secret, like he is protecting her. Feels like it is one last thing he can do for her, honouring and protecting her in death as he had always tried to do in life. She had a lot of secrets, secrets she never had the nerve to share. Secrets she would never have wanted to be exposed in the harsh light of day. Some things are private, Earl reasons. What harm would there be in one more secret for Ella? For this reason Earl chooses to tell no-one, not his brother, not Grace or Ben, not Frank.

Frank and Earl have grown apart and now have very little in common yet Frank has been a good companion to Earl through these most troubled days. They hang out and drink beer together for three days and talk about some of their happier childhood times together with Prince.

On the third day Frank drives Earl to the impound yard where the remains of Ella's car have been towed. It is the worst thing Earl has ever seen. The car is an unrecognizable mass of twisted metal. Earl wants only to be alone after that because he isn't sure how to react and doesn't know what to do with all of the anger and sadness erupting inside of him. It feels like the complete demolition of his heart.

He does not know his own emotions or his own heart, it is all dreadfully foreign and bewildering. What should he feel; rage, regret, acceptance? With uneasy footing he searches his soul for answers and finds that all this is what he might have expected had he allowed himself the liberty to really think about it. Frank stays with him like a shadow. For three nights he sleeps on Earl's couch in the darkness of his living room, and never leaves his friend alone.

Grace and Ben handle the details of the service, mostly Grace. She arranges a small memorial in a room at the funeral home. Nothing preachy or over laden with religion. Just some short words about Ella's struggles in life and how she was overcoming the troubles of her past. Ella's internment follows the service. Her cremated remains are saved in a white porcelain urn. The urn is solemnly lowered into a nondescript gravesite beneath a maple tree in a little country cemetery on the outskirts of town.

Grace invites everyone who has attended the service to a gathering at her home afterwards. Sandwiches and coffee are served to a small handful of people. Ella's family and coworkers share a few stories and memories and finger sandwiches but most find that there is very little to say. Some comment that it was a lovely service. They drink their coffee in haste and pass on second cups. Most leave early.

Earl was completely sober all day that day, but deeply bothered later that he remembered very little about any of the details of the day. It all seemed to blend together in a distressingly intoxicating haze. He wished he could have done more to make the memory of the day more lasting but it was over without much ceremony.

In the days that followed Ella's funeral there really was very little for Earl to do. He was given two weeks leave from work but longed for the distractions that work would have provided. After the first week there was nothing left to do at all. The service was over, his brother had handled all the paper work, and Frank, Art, and Ben had all left. Frank went back to the city for college, Art and his wife returned to their own life. Ben returned to his work in the oil patch. Without his mother in the dark little house Earl feels absolutely abandoned.

CHAPTER THIRTY FOUR

EARL TRIES TO RAMBLE around the empty house he had shared with his mother. This only results in days spent sitting in the darkness of the living room where Ella had spent so many desperately lonely hours. Impatient for relief from this disparity Earl loads his quad, some hunting gear, and Prince into his truck. He drives the familiar road towards the broken down cabin where he and Ben often went to hunt.

The dirt roads are worn and familiar to him now, like an old pair of blue jeans. The golden kiss of Autumn only just beginning to show on the cool underbelly of the poplar woodlands and on the green waves of wheat and oats in the fields along the way. Earl feels a light gladness as he travels out of the confinements of town and a relief in the stillness of the early morning world as nature unfolds around him. Although the weather has cooled he rolls down the truck window to take in the fragrant aroma of ripening canola field blossoms. As he turns down this road, then that one, the familiar rolling hills seem to be calling out to him a soft and peaceful welcome. He has always felt a strong connection to the country and to the sights and sounds and smells of nature.

He has driven about half an hour when something new catches his eye. On the side of the road a sign, bright and new at the edge of a long winding driveway. The sign reads "for sale by owner, call Gerald", with a phone number at the bottom written with green felt marker. Earl turns in and drives up the driveway as if compelled by an inner encouragement.

There on the side of the gently sloping hill, at the end of the long drive, is a small rustic log house and open yard site. The backdrop of the tall forest makes the buildings appear small, but the expansive view of the valley that stretches out before the yard is something to behold. A colourful work of art by God's hand. Rolling fields and thick mossy forests as far as the eye can see.

A warm summer breeze blows through the yard as Earl steps from his truck to look around. Prince follows at his heels. The two main buildings are log, gray with age. There is a garage big enough to fit his truck and quad. Two small plywood sheds are discovered hidden behind the garage, nestled together in the shade of the tall trees. The log house looks sturdy but small. Earl steps up onto the porch and tries the front door. Finding it unlocked, he enters.

Inside the house is open and inviting, looking larger than it appears from the outside. A welcoming stone fireplace draws his appreciation in the living room. The kitchen is bright and spacious with space for the dinner table in the middle of the room. A short dim hall leads the way to two bedrooms, the bathroom, a utility room with laundry appliances, and a small boot room and storage space near the back door.

Earl walks back through the house from back to front making sure to close the front door on his way out. Stopping once more on the front porch Earl spies two wooden kitchen chairs worn with age stacked against the wall. He tugs them apart and sets one near the front door. He sits, Prince heals at his side and leans into his denim clad leg.

Sitting there Earl thinks to himself that he could spend all his time right there. He imagines watching the sunrise, morning coffee in hand, in this very spot and closing his day right here with a cold beer.

Earl stays a long hour in the old chair picturing his furniture in the rooms behind him and a rocking chair or two out here on the porch. He day dreams about waking up in the house and spending his weekends in the yard with Prince or in the garage where he might work on maintenance of his truck. Sitting there on the step he picks out a spot in the yard where the dog house will be placed at the side of the house. He imagines it will be nice to invite Grace and Ben to visit him here with little Ben.

In time Earl stands, stretches, and walks down the driveway with his dog at his side. He leaves his truck in the yard parked in front of the log house. When he gets to the road he takes a seldom used cell phone out of his shirt pocket and dials the phone number on the sign.

"Hello, Gerald? I'm calling about the house." After a short conversation Gerald agrees to meet Earl there in thirty minutes. This is coincidently the same Gerald who owns the Dodge Charger that Earl had recently worked on. Earl is gladdened to know a friendly face will meet with him here today.

The house had belonged to Gerald's uncle Paul. Paul had lived here for many years but passed away last winter. He had willed the small acreage to his much loved nephew, Gerald. Gerald lives on a ranch of his own with his daughter and has no need of the little log cabin. Gerald's home is back towards town a few miles, not far beyond the little country church that Earl had passed on his morning drive.

Earl and Prince walk back to the house and sit again on the porch to wait. In the waiting his thoughts go to his mother and the note she had left. "You will at least have that". He knew she was referring to insurance money, money that he would never see if they knew her death was a suicide. It could help to buy him this home, he would at least have that. He was more than ready for a new start in a home of his own. He feels like a rebirth could happen at any age, like he is starting over on a new first day.

The word "home" lingers warm on his heart until he has to say it out loud. Looking down at the loyal dog at his feet he rolls the word from his lips a few times. "Home...... home..... home."

Prince looks intently back at him, wags his tail and gives a little woof in reply.

Earl leans back in his chair comfortably as he waits for Gerald. He wonders about fate and karma and things he knows little about. He wonders about the other farms he had passed on his morning travels, neighbours. Briefly he returns inside the house and searches for signs of a basement door or hatch, finding none he returns to the step. With renewed satisfaction he leans his chair against the wall beneath the bare light bulb between the kitchen window and the front door and scratches Prince behind the ears.

He can't help but smile as he looks out over the valley before him with an inner appreciation. It seems like for the first time in his life he feels like he is where he was meant to be. It is a new feeling from the turmoil of his childhood or the dark melancholy of living with his despondent mother. It is almost a dreamlike peace incomparable to anything he has ever known. As he waits for Gerald he feels certain that he has finally found a home to call his own.

CHAPTER THIRTY FIVE

EARL HAS NEVER BEEN one for celebrating holidays. He doesn't like having to eat in a room full of people. He always preferred to eat alone without scrutinizing watchers or the tension of having the perception of an audience. He knows he has developed this inclination from the time in which Harold was a part of his life. That time is long past now. This time is different than any before. This time Earl can make his own rules. Earl's first and only rule is there will be no making rules.

It is Thanksgiving and he has a new sense of thankfulness this year. The incident with James almost a month earlier has changed him. Not on the outside, outside he is still the same quiet man. He wears the same blue jeans and drives the same old truck. Inside Earl feels stronger, feels needed, feels like he has something to give and someone to give to, a sense of family. This new sense of belonging changes everything.

He has telephoned his brother Art earlier in the week, it is the first time that they talk in months. It feels really good to him to hear the familiar voice of his brother. Time and distance has wedged a large divergence between them since their mother's death. They normally would share a phone call on special occasions but rarely have their conversations extended beyond that limited and disconnected relationship. Earl is newly hopeful that this pattern in their brotherhood might also change.

Now they have planned this reunion. Art and his wife are flying up to celebrate Thanksgiving with him. They are bringing their children. Earl's niece and nephew now twenty and sixteen years old.

Earl works tirelessly to prepare for his brother and his family's coming.

He even borrows his boss's motor-home for them all to stay in. It is large and spacious with a slide out living room. He parks it beside the house for them, fills the water hold and the fuel tank for the heater. He stocks it with groceries and bedding, it is very difficult for him to hide his growing anticipation. He even has Amber over to clean his house before their arrival in exchange for some manual work, repairs he carries out on her barns and fences.

Things with Amber are changing in subtle ways also. He has never been very good with the opposite sex, blames the drinking and work although secretly never feels he has the skills or confidence in any social situation. Lately he finds himself flirting with his neighbour and friend. It isn't the wild pick up lines or come-on's he sees other men succeed with, just little gestures and timid fleeting touches.

It makes him smile inside and out when Amber bashfully and discretely smiles back. Sometimes she only smiles with her eyes but it warms him just the same, and the last two Sundays Amber has sat next to him at church where it was ok for his leg to awkwardly rest against hers as they listen to the weekly sermon.

Inside Earl is wanting to take things very slow because it is all somewhat intimidating and in a way very unfamiliar. He doesn't see her every day but he thinks of her much more often now. He finds that he likes the way she smells at church, day dreams about her long blonde hair, and wonders about how to compliment her with out it sounding too uncomfortably dorky. It always seems a little dorky to him.

Friday before Thanksgiving Earl goes to the airport to pick up his brother Art and his wife and kids. To their astonishment he greets everyone with a big affectionate hug and carries the children's luggage to the truck himself. On the drive to his home Earl is more talkative than Art can ever recall, chattering about Ben and James, Amber, and Gerald. Even boring with them with stories about his twenty years of work at the automotive shop. They reconnect over a barbeque supper in the front yard and close the day drinking beers on the step as they look out over the rolling valley now vibrant in Autumns glorious pallet. Earl is extremely proud to be sharing this weekend at his home with his family.

Saturday morning Gerald comes over and takes Earl and Art out hunting. They drive out to the cabin on the quads. It is a journey of discovery as Earl and Art learn that they are both very accomplished hunters although they had never actually hunted together. It is a day of stories, fishing on the river bank, and beers around a camp fire. The excursion lasts until night fall.

Sunday is Thanksgiving and there is much preparations to do in the morning. A huge Thanksgiving dinner is planned and Earl is excited for the day. He tidies his house with a whistle on his lips. His sister-in-law and niece help prepare food in Earl kitchen in the morning before church. Art and his son are given directions to a local campground from where they will "borrow" two picnic tables for the day. David arrives at his mother Amber's home early with a girlfriend, bringing fresh baked fruit pies. Amber slides her roasting pan containing a large stuffed turkey into her oven before leaving home for church. Gerald packs his old beat up guitar and his daughter off to Sunday service. Pete and Elsie are invited and have prepared traditional Polish foods for the feast, cabbage rolls and perogies. All are excited for the dinner they are planning but none more than Earl.

CHAPTER THIRTY SIX

"Look dad...." James calls from where he is sitting at the kitchen table. "I can spell my name. J...A...M...E...S."

Ben comes to the kitchen to see his little boys efforts. Across a white sheet of loose leaf paper in shaky blue crayon five large letters fill the page.

"That is really good work James," He pats the boy's shoulder. "Look how much you can do after only a short time of first grade."

"My teacher says I'm a fast learner and I know all my colors and I can count all the days on the calendar."

"Yeah I know, she told me you are learning your numbers and shapes too and the bus driver told me you learned all the bus rules. You should be very proud James, I know I am." Ben pats his son on the shoulder before he pours himself a second cup of coffee.

"One more cup of coffee and then we had best get ready for church. It's nice outside this morning, are you coming out to join me on the step?"

James gathers most of his papers and all of his crayons and puts them away in a drawer near the fridge. He uses a green alphabet magnet, the W, to put the page with his name on the fridge door next to the word FRIDGE.

At the start of the school year Ben put name labels on almost every item in the house; fridge, table, door, window,..... etcetera. He remembered how his mother, Grace, had done this for him when he was in first grade and how Earl had sometimes helped him with those words. He thinks it is a good family tradition and James is fast learning the alphabet the same way his father did and spelling many small household words.

James carries his glass of apple juice outside, with a lazy yawn Jack gets up from under the kitchen table and follows. The boy sits next to his father on the front step in a child size lawn chair, there just for him. The morning air is brisk and sharp with the promise of colder days to come but the waking sunlight that stretches lazily across the early landscape before them breathes softly of warmth and brightness to come this Autumn day.

"Dad, is Uncle Earl coming over to visit today?"

"No, he's not coming here James. We will see him at church. It's Thanksgiving today and he has invited us to his home for Thanksgiving dinner. His brother's family came a very long way to visit, and Gerald and his daughter will be there, and Amber and David."

"Pete and Elsie too? I think they are like a grampa and gramma only different. Like uncle Earl is my uncle. Are they gonna be there?"

"Yes, Pete and Elsie too."

"Teacher told me about thanksgiving. She said that people have nice dinners for Thanksgiving like the first Thanksgiving. Are we having a nice dinner today."

"Yes we are son. Not here in our home, at Earl's home."

The word home hangs in the air like a warm mist. Not just a roof over their heads, but a feeling of comfort and belonging that wasn't there before. They have Earl to thank for this. Ben can not imagine where they would be right now without Earl's help and support over the hardships of the summer.

"Dad? How come we never had church before?"

"I guess we just didn't have time. Things were always busy before. That's how I remember it. Life was busy in the city and now it is slower, more relaxed. I'm glad we have church now. I'm glad you showed it to me and I'm glad Earl showed it to you."

"Is being glad like being thankful?"

"Yes, exactly."

"Then I'm glad too Dad."

CHAPTER THIRTY SEVEN

THE SUN RISES HIGH in the warm Sunday sky and the congregation hums with an anxious buzz. It is a joyful feeling to be here but everybody in the crowd seems restless also and eager to get on with their day. They come out of a sense of obligation and some believe it to be an important part in their Thanksgiving day plans but regardless of the reasons they all seem impatient for the sermon to finish so that they can get to other activities for this day. There are a lot of extra people here today also. Pews are packed with the regular local parishioners and also many visiting families and friends.

James and Ben arrived and sit next to Amber and David and David's girlfriend. They normally sit with Earl but today Earl's pew is filled with the faces of his visiting family. Gerald and his daughter join Earl also, but then Gerald gives up his seat to someone's visiting Grandma and stands at the back of the room.

The sermon is about the reasons for giving thanks and about who to thank in our lives. James fades, eyelids fluttering, he misses the story. Wakes up in time to put his two dollar coin in the collection plate, a carved maple bowl with red velvet lining that makes a thud when the heaviness of the coin drops into it. The congregation sings "I know that my redeemer lives….", eyelids flutter. He wakes in time for lemonade and sandwiches.

After church a short caravan of pick-up trucks leaves the church yard. They form a train heading West on the dirt roads towards Earl's house. Ben turns off at his own house to get Jack. He also gets James' bicycle which recently has had the training wheels removed. Ben goes to the kitchen to get a potato salad and beers from the fridge. This is his contribution to the pot luck meal. Then they are back in the truck going down the road to Earl's house.

Earl's yard is a sunny bustle of activity. Gerald is unloading his quad from his truck box. The women are setting the picnic tables with dishes and an abundance of food and drinks. Pete and Art are sitting in lawn chairs having beers while Pete teaches Art's son chords on an old guitar. Art's daughter and Gerald's daughter are driving around Earl's yard together on Earl's quad. Amber arrives and goes directly to the kitchen with the hot turkey straight from her oven, the aroma of the birds wafting through the air in her wake.

Ben parks his truck in the shade of the trees and unloads his son and the puppy from the cab first, then the bicycle from the box, then the salad which he promptly hands off to Elsie on her way to the house. Earl greets him with a beer and an unexpected bear hug. Recently realizing new hopes for his future and freedom from past shames Earl's actions are becoming unhindered, less reserved, and more expressive.

"What was that for?" Ben asks.

"It's a thank you. Thank you Ben for everything you've done for me. Just thanks for being part of my family." He steps back and kneels to hug James as well. "Thank you too James." He stands and takes a drink from his beer, neglects to brush the dust from the knees of his blue jeans.

"It's us who should be thanking you, Earl. I can honestly say we would be lost without you and everything you have done for us and given us. You've given us family, you have no idea how big a deal it is for us, for me and James to have that."

Earl hugs Ben again. "Yes, Ben I have an idea. I have an idea about family. I might not have that without the love you mother showed me when I was a boy not much older than James. I wouldn't be doing right by her if I didn't take that love and pay it forward. It feels like the right thing to do. I think your mom is likely looking down and smiling today."

"You saying that means the world to me Earl." The two men stand in silence a moment as the little boy gets on his bicycle and rides, his shadow wobbling beside him. Jack runs along side and nips at the shadow in the dust. Ben and Earl stand and watch a while and wordlessly sip from their beer cans. They both smile and laugh as they watch the bike rider teeter proudly down the driveway without the aid of training wheels.

"Come on," Earl says at length. "lets join the rest of the family." And in his heart he means it… the word "family", they are all his family. Some by blood and some by choice. All family in his heart.

The remains of the day evolves in a joyful conglomeration of food and song and friendship and laughter. The meal fills their bellies and the fellowship warms every heart. New connections are made over dinner and old bonds are renewed.

As evening approaches Earl reflects about the turning points in his life. It isn't the bright carefree days that come to mind, it is the stormy weather that has made him deeply aware of his blessings.

Of course sunny days matter, and fair weather friends are still friends to be counted, but those friends stand unremarkable and those days often fade in his memories. What has really come to matter to Earl are times full of clouds and overcast. The people that matter are the one that show up at your side when storms are brewing. Names flood his thoughts as he considers the darkest of his days; his mother Ella, Grace, Gerald, his teacher from long ago Mark Carlson, Ben and James.

Not one for words, Earl has never shared his appreciation of those special people in his life until now. Ben had never known before but he is an enormous part of this honoured group, more so than he could imagine. In the darkest days of Earl's youth the infant Ben, little Ben, had been a ray of hope and a remarkable cause for inspiration in what was otherwise hopeless and difficult times. Earl's greatest honour is to repay Ben in some small way by anchoring Ben through his own recent dark times.

As the sun begins to sink low in the evening sky and the bright autumn colors fade so do the activities of the day. Dishes are cleared away and chairs are gathered to the steps of Earl's home. Ben turns on the porch light and Pete and Gerald softly strum their Guitars and hum folksy gospel songs. Women play cards in the kitchen and men drink their beers on the step. James climbs up into his uncle Earl's lap and nods off to sleep as Earl gently rocks his rocking chair back and forth in time with the music. Jack curls up under Art's chair, the tired puppy almost instantly asleep.

CHAPTER THIRTY EIGHT

BEN WALKS THE LENGTH of the driveway to the end where James has abandoned his bicycle hours earlier to pursue other endeavours with Jack. The sun is almost gone from the Autumn sky and the fall colours fade into darkness around him. The bike is small and light weight, he carries it easily as he strolls back towards the house.

Beyond the house Ben's eyes travel upward, beyond the deepening darkness of the tree line. The day is closing. It was a good day, the best of days in recent memory, but Ben is also glad for it to be ending. Lavender grey clouds stretch thin against the dying blue sky as a creamy marigold moon whispers it's contrast against the disappearing warmth of the setting sun. The trees below the moon are dark and poetic. The house is nestled in the shadows, lamp lit windows beckoning him closer towards Earl's home and the family still gathered there on the step.

At first Ben's focus is drawn to the bright porch light near the door. Then as his strides carry him closer his eyes are fondly drawn to his child. James is peacefully asleep in Earl's arms in the warm shadows of Earl's home. In seeing them Ben's heart fills with the strong protective love of a father.

Ben recalls a little of what he knows about Earl's childhood and about the relationship that Earl had with his mother Grace. He remembers his mother had helped Earl recover from a dark time in his life just as Earl now helped him and his son. A scripture comes to his thoughts and since Ben is not well versed in the Bible the clarity of this verse in his mind is a surprise to him. He recites the words in a whisper only he will hear.

"If I say "Surely the darkness will hide me and the light become night around me." even the darkness will not be dark to you; the night will shine like the day, for darkness is as light to you."

To the best of his memory he thinks that the verse is from the book of Psalms. He utters the words softly again as his focus remains lovingly on Earl and James and the others who are bathed in the soft glow from the porch light.

The evening sky is gently darkening and the air is a warm a comfort as he slows his stroll towards the house and towards his friends and family gathered there. If the comfort of the rocking chair were closer to the brightness of the light bulb the child might not sleep. If not for Pete and Gerald's soft guitar melody Earl might not be rocking the child so gently in his arms. If the sun still blazed above....., well, it is plain to see that this is not a scene to exist in the brightness of any midday heat. It is comfortably cool, and tempered by shadows, and in Ben's heart it is remarkable.

ABOUT THE AUTHOR

I BELIEVE MY WRITING is a reflection of beliefs and personal influences that have gotten under my skin,those rare and precise moments that take root and stretch far beyond their inception. The parallels of human experiences and the profound commonness of all things, all voices, all joy and heartache. I find that the blank page is the best place for me to find perspective.

I am inspired by artists, authors, poets, and musicians who's essence is felt through their craft and in the art of poetic story telling. I make every effort to educate myself in writing by studying the works of other writers. Being able to share my work is a remarkable opportunity and privilege.

Thanks to family and to friendships which time and tragedy may not dissuade, accordingly I write.

CPSIA information can be obtained at www.ICGtesting.com
Printed in the USA
LVOW090115200911

246960LV00001B/5/P

9 781456 749798